TUMBLEWEED

Tumbleweed is a man forever on the move, driven by hate to find the man who killed his family and his young wife. Six years he has been hunting, and now down in San Paulo, he has at last found the evidence he's been searching for.

As he rides into town little does he know that he is soon to become embroiled in a mystery that involves a bank-robber, a double-crossing sheriff and an Indian girl. Furthermore, who is Lee Cherrill and why will he kill to hide his identity?

TUMBLEWEED

TUMBLEWEED

by

Tex Larrigan

Dales Large Print Books
Long Preston, North Yorkshire,
BD23 4ND, England.

British Library Cataloguing in Publication Data.

Larrigan, Tex
   Tumbleweed.

A catalogue record of this book is
available from the British Library

ISBN   1-84262-272-2 pbk

First published in Great Britain 1994

Cover illustration by arrangement with Norma Editorial

The right of Tex Larrigan to be identified as the author of this
work has been asserted by him in accordance with the
Copyright, Designs and Patents Act, 1988

Published in Large Print 2003 by arrangement with
Robert Hale Ltd.

Dales Large Print is an imprint of Library Magna Books Ltd.

Printed and bound in Great Britain by
T.J. (International) Ltd., Cornwall, PL28 8RW

ONE

He slammed down the empty glass on the long bar top of the Golden Garter saloon and turned to leave. He was tired. It had been a long ride from Howards Creek. He was conscious of his smell and was in two minds whether to eat or take a long overdue bath. His belly rumbled. The chink down the street would have to put up with the stink. He'd eat first and soak later.

The batwings crashed behind him as he stepped outside on to the shaded veranda and was just in time to watch a heavily loaded wagon roll in from the north. It had come far for the horses were dusty and lathered. His glance at the driver was cursory for beside him sat the most voluptuous woman he'd seen in his life, and he'd seen quite a few.

He drew in a deep breath, hunger forgotten in a sudden surge of naked lust. Chre – ist! He'd been out on the trail so long he'd forgotten how it could be. He swallowed hard as she waited for the young driver to

7

get down and help her alight.

She smiled at the gathering crowd showing white, even teeth in a demure but provocative fashion. Her hair was long and black and her brown eyes twinkled in the smooth brown face. She was Mexican and the boy looked to be her brother.

The man frowned. There was something not right for an observer of his experience. He watched as the boy produced a battered guitar and began to play. The girl twirled her body and began to dance in the dust of the street. Her red and white frilled blouse was low cut and showed her bosom. She should have been wearing a flounced skirt to match but she wasn't. She was wearing an old pair of men's pants. Intrigued, he stepped down and walked to the back of the crowd to inspect the wagon and its contents. He was surprised to find that it was filled with all the hardware that a peddling salesman would carry such as nails and wire and coffee-pots and frying pans. A rather curious collection for Mexicans to be sure!

The crowd cheered and stamped their feet and clapped their hands to the quickening tempo of the guitar. A quick look at the gyrating girl assured him that she was no pedlar's daughter. Her dancing was that of a professional. Walking farther round the wagon he saw the two tethered horses and he drew in a sharp astonished breath. These were no common mustangs but well-cared for riding horses and if he knew horses, they both had a touch of the Arabian in them. He ran his hand down the fetlock of the nearest. The muscles from shoulders to ankles were firm. He judged that the horse was used to long hard riding with stamina of a long line of ancestors brought up on oats and good breeding.

Again he glanced through the crowd at the girl dancing. He saw that she had the full attention of the male population and also that of the town's whores who were snarling insults for the loss of interest shown them.

He fingered the supple reins and cast a questing hand over soft well-cared-for saddle straps and glanced sharply at the blanket carelessly covering the butt of a rifle thrust deep into its boot. Hell! Those horses were ready for business!

He returned to his former pitch, wondering who the horses belonged to. It was strange and he felt a chill up his back. The fools watching had no thoughts beyond watching the girl's undulating buttocks. He was feeling the effect of them himself.

Already silver dollars were being flung at her feet. There was going to be a good take before she was through.

He smiled cynically. Already he could guess who would be the first in the queue. The tall feller with the expensive store suit and the big cigar looked to be in the running. It certainly wouldn't be him. He'd been caught fair on the hop. He should have washed up before going to the saloon for his drinks.

He was cursing his luck when four riders leisurely rode in from the south. The crowd were so excited what with the dancing and what they were imagining and the stirring rhythm of the guitar that none turned to watch the strangers pass by ... all except the drifter called Tumbleweed who eyed them narrowly as they tethered their horses outside the feed store next to the bank.

For a moment they all stopped to watch the woman and her dancing. Then quietly they went into the bank and Tumbleweed knew! The woman and the youth were decoys!

Moving quietly, Tumbleweed stepped back into the saloon hardly moving the batwings to do so. Inside, he checked his Colt and slapped bullets into the breech. His instinct was to be ready. He was sure he wasn't wrong. He watched through the window and counted the seconds. Any minute now...

He wasn't wrong. They came out blasting. Suddenly the woman and the youth both had weapons in their hands. It was pandemonium. Men yelled and women screamed and Tumbleweed plunged through the batwings and risked a shot above the heads of the crowd as the four men thundered by. His eyes swivelled to the woman but she was fanning her gun and moving backwards towards the rear of the wagon and the tethered horses. The boy was already springing lightly into the saddle. He straightened and fired two shots in quick succession as he covered the woman's withdrawal. Now she was shouting orders and Tumbleweed, who was drawing a bead on the youth, lowered his weapon. After all, it was no business of his. He was here on far more important business than that of winging a stranger on a bank raid.

He watched the two riders as they kicked up dust along Main Street and on out of town. San Paulo had seen the last of them, that was for sure. He wondered again about the wagon. He thought it prudent to take a look. The townsfolk had not yet thought about the wagon. Most of them were

11

running in the wake of the riders and screaming abuse and shaking futile fists.

This time Tumbleweed looked in the front of the wagon. It was dim inside and it smelled of coal oil and wagon-wheel grease and coffee beans and the stink of a man who hadn't washed in months. He wrinkled his nose. Surely he didn't smell as bad as that?

Suddenly he grasped the side of the wagon and heaved himself inside. The smell was now overpowering. Back in the shadows he'd seen movement and there were sounds like that of a kitten miaowing. Colt drawn, he moved in a crouch to take a looksee.

He stared down at a scrawny, bloodied figure trussed up like a turkey jock who blinked up at him, while gulping sounds issued from behind a gag.

'Just a minute, old-timer, you'll soon be free.' Tumbleweed took his knife and cut the bonds tying the wrists. Then without cere-mony, he yanked the gag free taking some of the old man's sparse moustache with it.

There came a howl of rage and pain.

'God dammit! Must you be so bloody rough?' he yelped. 'You're as bad as those bastards! God damn them to hell!'

Tumbleweed shrugged.

'You wanted freeing. What happened?'

'They pulled me up two hours from town. Said they wanted to buy a sack of coffee. When I turned to get it, one of the varmints cold-cocked me and when I woke up I was gagged and a young Mex and a woman were whipping hell out of the horses. I sure thought the wagon would keel over. If I could get my hands on them I'd...'

Tumbleweed broke in on the tirade.

'Do you know who they were?'

'Not the young 'uns. I heard the Mex kid mention a feller called Lee Cherrill but the woman shut him up real smart. The devil's curse on them! I've got a head that feels as if it's been scalped!'

Tumbleweed helped him to sit upright. The old-timer groaned and rocked and Tumbleweed steadied him.

'Any rotgut? You could sure use a snort.'

The old drummer pointed a shaking finger at a trapdoor let into the bed of the wagon.

'I keep some bottles under there along with my money. I hope you can keep your mouth shut, mister.'

'Sure, I'm no blab-mouth.' He quickly pulled up the boards and produced a bottle of whiskey and offered it.

Two good pulls and wheezing a little he offered it to Tumbleweed.

13

'Jesus! How I needed that! Do you want a pull?'

Tumbleweed looked at the slavering, twitchy mouth and decided he didn't need a drink. He wanted grub instead. He shook his head.

'You have it, mister. Your need is greater than mine.'

'Well now, you've been real kindly, stranger. I think I'll have another pull and then I'll get me all hitched up and get me to the livery barn and get these horses of mine some feed and water. The poor beasts took some punishment and they be good friends of mine!'

'You're sure you're OK?'

'Yep. It's only a crack on the head. I'll live, I reckon.'

'Then I'm going to find some chuck. I might see you later.'

The old man rubbed his head and watched him go, liking the well-set up figure, the set of shoulders and the air of watchful command. Not a man to tangle with. Coming to that conclusion, he set about his business. He hadn't been robbed, only used. The varmints had needed his wagon to create a diversion while the real business went on. He was lucky he'd only got a crack over the head. He could have

14

been crowbait by now.

Tumbleweed paused outside the saloon. Some townsfolk were still talking excitedly in small groups. One larger group attracted his interest. He moved forward to listen, recognizing that the tall, gaunt man sporting a tin star was the law in these parts and that he was having a bad time. He was scowling at a small overweight man dressed in black store clothes. He was obviously the banker and the weedy individuals hanging around him were his tellers.

'I tell you, Hawkins, it's not good enough! This is the second time in three months the bank's been cleaned out. What the hell do we pay you for if you can't anticipate a robbery? My associates are not going to like this latest raid. They're going to feed me to the crows! What are you going to do about it?'

'What do you think I can do, Mister Shawcross? Same as last time. Send out my deputies and hope for the best. I'll look up the Wanted posters and see if there's anything on the woman. She might give us a lead.'

'Like hell you will! She'll be long gone before you get a posse organized. Whoever heard of a woman outlaw in this territory? No, she was brought in for this one job, mark my words. Someone knew there was

15

extra cash deposited for Ted Ramsey's shipment of beeves...'

Tumbleweed raised his head. Ted Ramsey ... and the raucous voice of the banker faded as Tumbleweed once again allowed the name of Ramsey to fill his mind and bridge the gap of six long years. So he was on the right track at last!

Again he relived the pain of his homecoming. He closed his eyes and shivered, the stench of woodsmoke and spilled blood again in his nostrils. He'd been two hours behind Quantrill and his gang and there had been nothing left but smouldering ruins, the corpses of his parents and his young wife and his dying kid brother who'd lived long enough to give him the name of Quantrill's lieutenant before he died. Edward George Ramsey! The bastard who took over the gang when Quantrill died in '65 and turned the once crack Confederate platoon into a rabble with whom even the James brothers refused to ride. Ted Ramsey, the man Tumbleweed had been trailing for six years!

Quickly Tumbleweed stepped forward and touched the brim of his hat in greeting as the paunchy little man looked him over.

'Sir, I couldn't but help overhear what was said, and I saw what happened. Can I offer my services?'

Bud Hawkins raised his stained stetson and scratched a sweaty forehead, thankful for a respite, then mopped his brow.

'And who the hell are you? I haven't seen you in these parts before!' The beefy little man's eyes raked Tumbleweed up and down with a faint insolence that made him want to smack him on the jaw.

'I rode in less than an hour ago. As you see, I haven't had time to wash up. But if you want a man capable of going after that gang...' he paused, and then went on softly, 'as you see, I'm harnessed up for bear!'

Banker Shawcross took in the two tied-down Colts and nodded.

'You as good with your left as well as your right?'

'Better. I'm left-handed.'

'Huh! That doesn't say much!'

'No?' Suddenly there was a swift flowing movement and two scavenging crows fluttered to the ground, black feathers blowing everywhere.

Tumbleweed smiled at the reactions from those around him. He blew down both barrels before looping the weapons back into their holsters. 'Now, what about it?'

The banker screwed up his eyes, his

piercing stare shrewd and assessing.

'Why do you want to get mixed up in our troubles, mister?'

Tumbleweed shrugged. 'Money. I'm broke. Rode in here to find me a job. I might as well work for you as any other man. Take the offer or leave it. I don't care a shit!'

He turned to walk away. His belly thought his throat was cut. If the flabby little banker didn't want him, he could look up Ted Ramsey himself and bugger the gang, except that he would have liked to meet the woman again. She was some looker and she certainly made his juices flow...

'Hey, now, just a minute. Not so fast. I didn't say I wasn't interested. I'm just curious, is all. Now come inside and have a drink and we'll discuss terms.'

'What about our friend, the sheriff here? Doesn't he have a say?'

Shawcross smiled. 'Hawkins? Oh, he does what I say. I'm head of the town committee. I see he gets paid for his job. You want this here gunman as one of your deputies, don't you, Sheriff?' He put a hearty hand on Hawkins' shoulder.

Hawkins coughed and spat and then looked at Tumbleweed.

'Yeh,' he mumbled. 'I didn't catch your

18

name, feller?'

'I didn't give it,' Tumbleweed said easily. 'I'm known as Tumbleweed.'

'Haven't you a goddam proper name?' the banker asked irascibly.

'My name is my own private affair,' Tumbleweed answered coldly. 'Take it or leave it.'

'Oh, so you're one of them. Not on the run, are you? You haven't the gall to come here and get taken on as a deputy and you're on a Wanted poster yourself?'

'Nope. I wouldn't be in this neck of the woods if I was a wanted man. I'd be over the border to hell and gone!'

'Huh! Well, Tumbleweed or whatever your name is, you've got a job, so come in and have a drink and you too, Hawkins, and let us all get acquainted.'

Tumbleweed grinned at the scowling Hawkins. He knew that the sheriff was feeling humiliated. He didn't blame him. If he'd been sheriff, he too would have balked at the fat banker's high-handed way of taking on another deputy.

There would be time later to make his peace with the old lawman when the banker wasn't around.

Two hotshots later, Tumbleweed was

feeling the lack of grub. His guts rebelled at the raw whiskey and, as he wiped his mouth on the back of his hand, he was conscious that his tongue was beginning to run away with him.

'Well now, it's time I went and found me some chow. See you in a piece, Sheriff, and good day to you, Mr Shawcross, sir.' Tumbleweed nodded in the banker's direction.

'Not so fast, mister. We haven't settled on rates. I like a binding contract, mister. What are you prepared to do to earn your money?'

Tumbleweed looked him in the eye and Shawcross shivered at the haunted ice-cold stare and was glad they were on the same side.

'I'll do whatever has to be done. Have no fear of that, Mr Shawcross and I'll expect top rates if I bring back stiffs. I'm not your pet sheriff, Mr Shawcross.' Now he let the beginnings of a sneer colour his voice.

'What are you, feller, a bounty-hunter?'

'Nope. Just a drifter who's willing to do a dirty job!'

With that, he stood up and hitched his pants and made his way through the bat-wings of the saloon.

Shawcross watched him go and then looked uncertainly at the silent Hawkins.

'I'm not sure about that *hombre*. We might have caught a tiger by the tail.'

'Yeh, boss, and a tail we might not find it so easy to let go!'

Shawcross nodded. 'Watch him, Hawkins. Let him do the dirty work. If rumour's right and Cherrill is with that gang, we'll need his help. We've got to get those bastards! Afterwards ... well, there's always other ways and means.' He gave a low laugh. Hawkins looked uncomfortable.

'Look, Mr Shawcross, we don't want any more violence. Last time the federal marshal came in and he gave me hell! We were lucky there wasn't a more thorough enquiry. If he comes in again we might not be so lucky.'

'Cut your snivelling, Hawkins, I know what I'm doing. You just do your job and I'll do mine.'

'Then we'll let that feller do what he has to do, and you pay him and let him ride out!'

'Huh! We'll see how he makes out.'

'I said you will pay him and let him ride out, Mr Shawcross.'

'Are you telling me what to do?'

'It sounds that way but I mean no offence. But I'm not standing for any more bushwhacking at the back of Molly's place.'

'Well, he'd better do a good job then. You'd

better send young Drydon with him and old Mort to make it look good. Keep the townsfolk happy.'

'I'll do that. They can be away at day-break.'

'No: give that feller time to eat and wash and clean his guns and then get them on their way.'

'But they can't see sign in the dark!'

'Use your head, feller. Sign up the half-breed. He can follow sign when he's blind drunk. You'll be doing old Bet a favour getting him out of town. She can join Molly and her girls as long as he's away; put a few dollars in one of her black stockings. She'll think kindly of you too, you old dog!'

Hawkins looked uncomfortable.

'For God's sake, don't joke. If the missis heard you...'

'Go on, you old goat! Everyone knows you sniff round Bet's petticoats and I bet your missis knows and keeps quiet. She knows a good sitting-down when she's found one. As long as she's got food in her belly and a roof over her head she's just like the rest. Women! All they want is security, damn them!'

He stomped out of the saloon. Pensively, Hawkins finished his drink and followed suit. He'd better round up Mort and young

Drydon and then he'd ride out to the half-breed's shack half a mile from town and swear the drunken swine in.

It was only when he was nicely aboard his old mare that his face relaxed. With a bit of luck he might see Bet. With a bit more luck Indian Tottie might be off somewhere and he would have to wait for him ... he was conscious of a tightness in his pants. By cripes, he wished his own wife had some of what Bet had, but on second thoughts, knew it would be a disaster. His thin, narrow-faced wife with the small, disapproving mouth and the bony body would never have what Bet had and gave so freely.

He jigged the mare to a faster trot.

TWO

Hawkins stared at the clean-shaven gunman. He hardly recognized him as the stinking hobo who'd been forced on him as a deputy. Gone were the sweat-stained levis, the torn black shirt and the grease daubed jerkin. The only familiar items about him were the well-oiled guns thrust deep into greased holsters.

He even sported a new stetson from the general store ... one of the more expensive ones with a snakeskin band. That proved he wasn't broke as he made out. The man was a liar. Still, he was Shawcross's headache if things went wrong.

He nodded tersely, picking his teeth with a sliver of wood.

'You took your time, bud. The other deputies are waiting in the saloon. Probably pissed by now. Young Drydon can't hold his liquor. The orders are that you're to get on your way, pronto.'

'Like hell! I'll move out when I'm good and ready. I've just soaked my arse and I'm not getting blisters to please that old coot. I don't suppose he's forked a horse in the last ten years. I'm having one night in bed, goddamit, before I hit trail.'

Hawkins shrugged.

'It was your idea, feller. No one twisted your arm to volunteer.'

'I'm doing the job, mister, but I'll do it my way. Now give me the lowdown on what goes on around here, and who is this Lee Cherrill and the woman and the kid?'

'We don't know much about the woman or the kid but Cherrill was one of Quantrill's guerrillas. By all accounts he's a big-headed bastard and has never met a man who would stand up to him. They say he can do some fancy shooting. He killed a Mex last year but it was no contest. The poor fool was more used to a pitchfork than a gun.'

'Why did he square up to him then?'

'Because the murdering bastard forced a gun on him, insulted his sister and took pot-shots at his feet until he was forced to draw and that was when Cherrill blew him away.'

'And you didn't go after him?'

Hawkins looked uncomfortable. 'Because he wasn't in my territory I'm pleased to say! He's not a man I hope to meet. Now you, by the look of them there guns might just take him on. I hope you find him and bring him back slung across his horse. He's worth five hundred dollars.'

'That so? Now about the others. Where do they hang out?'

'All I know is that they ride in from the south. Maybe they come from over the border. There's plenty of hole-up joints on the other side of the Rio Grande.'

'And what about Shawcross's associates that he's so goddammed worried about? Who are they?'

Hawkins shifted uncomfortably. 'I reckon I shouldn't talk about the boss's business.

All I can say is that they ride on his back and he rides on mine.'

'So, he's got your tongue, eh? Must have a mighty hold on you, Sheriff, if you can be loyal to a blustering pig-faced bully with the stink and manners of a hog!'

'Watch yourself, buster, or you'll be out of a job!'

Tumbleweed laughed heartily, his amusement genuine.

'That's good coming from you. You'd shit yourself if you had to head out yourself and trail those guys. So lay off. I'm just putting it on the line. I don't have to like that guy to work for him and I don't have to take petty orders. I work in my own way. Savvy? Now give me the name of those associates.'

'Why? What's so important about them?'

'I have my reasons. I want to know the overall picture. I don't want to go after that bunch and find I've got unknown enemies stalking my back!'

'Hell, they're only a bunch of businessmen and ranchers who mind their own business and take their dividends.'

'Not by the way Shawcross was bellowing. Now, names please.'

Hawkins chewed his lip and sighed. Then taking the view that Shawcross would know how to handle this awkward cuss if need be, he said hoarsely, 'Look if I tell you, you won't say I told you?'

Tumbleweed grinned. This joker was easy meat. 'Cross my heart. I can keep my mouth shut.'

'Then there's six of them, the big shots. The ones with the real money. There's a lot of little guys but they don't count. It's Tom Breckonby, Silas Harper and Josh Kipling who are the big financiers. They have their fingers in lots of pies. Most of Harper's money is in the railroads.'

'And the others?'

'They're the ranchers who have their own money tied up. Lend their surplus to their poorer neighbours and call in loans when times are hard. They're not popular in these parts. In fact, there's some folk who'll be real pleased when they hear of this latest robbery.'

'And their names, Sheriff? Quit stalling. I want their names.'

'Oh hell! There's Hans Mueller of the Flying M and Ted Ramsey of the TR Circled and William Bisset of the Bisset Cattle Corporation. All the ranches are situated west or north-west, well away from the direction the gang rode in from. I can't see...'

Tumbleweed grunted.

27

'Thanks Sheriff. It was sure like pulling teeth, getting information out of you. Now I'd better go and meet those guys of yours and put them straight as to who's running this show.'

As Hawkins predicted, old Mort and young Drydon were glassy-eyed and enjoying the sounds of their own voices. Tumbleweed noticed that the half-breed sat a little apart and listened. He drank sparingly. Mort told a story about Indian shooting in the old days. He talked as if he had been on a vermin-killing spree.

Tumbleweed glanced at the breed, but he wasn't giving anything away. His eyes remained blank when Tumbleweed introduced himself. This was a man to watch, Tumbleweed decided. He noticed however, that the breed's eyes fastened on the two strapped-down guns.

Old Mort, grey-haired and creaky round the edges had the experience of manhunting but he didn't look like a stayer. Now the young feller ... he could be a liability. What in hell was the sheriff playing at, giving him two such unlikely deputies? Surely the town could have produced two more likely lawmen?

The hairs on the back of Tumbleweed's

neck bristled. He could smell something fishy and as he sniffed it got worse. Hell, it didn't look as if Hawkins, or was it Shawcross, wanted the gang caught! Maybe there was some mighty funny game going on.

And maybe he'd made a God almighty fool of himself by volunteering his services in the first place. Maybe he should have stuck to his idea and gone after Ramsey. But now he was committed.

He ordered drinks all round and the men visibly relaxed. Then, looking about him he said softly, 'Anyone objecting to a stranger coming into town and taking over this posse had better leave now. We don't want animosity, now do we?'

Old Mort shifted his feet and pushed back his battered bowler hat and pulled at his beer.

'Anyone who provides free beer is my man no matter where he comes from. I'm with you.'

'And you?' – looking at young Drydon. He looked at Mort and the old man nodded.

'I'm with Mort. He took me in as a kid when my folks were killed by Indians. I do what he does.'

Tumbleweed nodded. 'What about you, mister?' – to the half-breed.

29

'Anyone who's willing to face Lee Cherrill is for me,' the man said softly. 'He strung up my paw and made him die real slow. I'd like to see him suffer!'

'Right. Then I take it you'll all take orders from me? Mr Shawcross has hired me personal to go after that gang, seeing as the sheriff has no guts for that kind of thing.'

Old Mort laughed. 'Stands to reason doesn't it? Hawkins wipes Shawcross's arse. He wouldn't like his pet sheriff to be too far away from him. Those two go back a long way. I reckon Shawcross owes Hawkins an easy living. He knows too much about him, I reckon.'

'Well, seeing all that's settled, we'd better get some shut-eye. We'll be off before day-break. I understand you're a good tracker,' he said turning to the breed. 'What is your name?'

The breed stared at him and Tumbleweed's impression that it was going to be a battle of wills in getting co-operation from this man solidified. He needed this man. He was a tracker and he knew this country like the back of his hand. Also he had contacts. No doubt he knew all the small pockets of Indians. He would be welcome in any lodge. He spread his hands in quiet acceptance.

'OK, buster, if you don't want to tell me...'

'Folks round here call me Tottie,' the breed answered sulkily. 'My Indian friends call me something else.'

'Fair enough, Tottie. You can call me Tumbleweed.' A thin smile crossed his face. 'I'm called something else back east, so we're quits. Shake, pal.' And he stuck out his fist.

Tottie grinned and suddenly the tension was all gone. They shook hands and Tumbleweed felt the little tickling sensation between his shoulder-blades disappear. If there had been going to be trouble it would have come from this man, not the oldster or the boy.

They were a morose bunch who gathered before dawn. Mort's head ached and Drydon wasn't sure whether he had a head at all. He was still green from the night before and he retched as he followed the others at a snail's pace. Only Tottie acknowledged Tumbleweed's terse greeting. He was already wondering what he had let himself in for.

'Which direction do you reckon we should take? They wouldn't keep on due south. They must have cut off somewhere along the way. What do you figure?'

Tottie sucked at his teeth.

'My reckoning is that they would cut away

through Coldstream Gorge. It's a shortcut to the border, if that was their intention. Maybe they expected pickings on the way. I think we should stick to the trail for a spell and, as soon as the sun comes up, we'll break trail and fan out until we cross sign. What d'you say, boss?'

'Yeh, might save us time and grief. Yeh, we'll do that.'

A nod and a muttered word to Mort and so they rode on until the first streaks of yellow and pink heralded a new day.

Tumbleweed chose Tottie to ride with for Mort had gradually come back to his own shrewd self after a couple of snorts of rotgut and was busy giving the tenderfoot Drydon a few pointers about posseing.

It was hard getting Tottie to talk for he was a good tracker and his mind and eyes were on the ground. But he did talk and Tumbleweed understood that Shawcross had the town sewn up tight. Most of the property in and around San Paulo was owned by the bank and that meant Shawcross and his associates who were something of a mystery. Tottie told of dirt farmers run off their properties and the land fenced off for the big spreads. Even he had suffered under Shawcross and lost his livery stable to one of

Shawcross's enforcers.

'Why do the townsfolk stand for it?'

Tottie shrugged.

'Because the big ranchers send in their crews and if anyone in town has voiced any objections on how the town is run then they have an accident, or their place goes up in flames. There's been bushwhackings and saloon fights and lots of harassment for the womenfolk and I'm not talking about the whores.'

'Sounds grim. Is there no leader amongst you?'

'Not now. Last guy who objected got knifed in the back.'

'What about this Ted Ramsey? Does he come into town?'

Indian Tottie gave him a measuring glance.

'Do you know Ramsey?'

'The sheriff mentioned him along with Mueller, and Bisset of the Cattle Corporation. Seemingly they're mixed up with Shawcross. They're supposed to be shareholders in the bank along with some money men from back east. Right?'

'As far as I know that's right. Don't know much about them there money men but I do know that the ranchers make Shawcross

33

jump through hoops. Mueller is a sharp bastard. His crew are the local enforcers. They eat the best food, drink the best whiskey and get the best women. They've even been after my Bet.' Tottie's eyes flashed. 'If someone ever forced her...'

'Yeh, what would you do?'

'Cut his balls off with a rusty knife!'

Tumbleweed nodded. The more he heard, the more he liked Tottie. He was a man after his own heart.

'What about Ramsey?'

'Ramsey? Never seen him. Never comes into San Paulo. His boys come in about twice a year and shoot the place up. His ranch is on the other side of the range, way back. He's the mystery man of the bunch. Of course there're rumours about him and what they do.'

'Like what?'

'Oh, running a crooked outfit. There was a breed running with them called Tommy Big Nose and we were friendly. One night he got pissed and started a brawl in the Golden Garter. He got thrown out and I got him to the livery barn and mopped him up. He told me the boss would go wild if he heard about the ruckus.'

'Do you think he would be kicked out?'

'Nope. Those boys know too much. Anyhow, he would have ridden into town. It's the nearest from the TR Circled. He's out there working for Ramsey and Ramsey will be paying him well for what he has to do.'

'What does he do?'

Tottie shrugged. 'Do you want to know what I know or what I think?'

'Both.'

'Well, Tommy's a wrangler. That's his job as such. But Tommy told me he helped with other jobs like moving small bunches of cattle into small canyons and grazing them until they put on beef. Some of the cattle appear to have walked themselves into the ground before being handed over. Ramsey would shoot Tommy if he knew how his mouth runs off. Now, what I think, is that Ramsey takes rustled cattle. He hides them out until they beef up and then passes them on to Bisset. Bisset has a rail junction on his land. No one in San Paulo knows what's going out in those cattle trucks of his. He's got it made.'

'And Mueller? You think he's supplying Bisset too?'

'Why not? Between them all, they own most of this county and what they don't own, Shawcross's bank does. They've got this part of the country sewn up.'

'Hm, and where does Cherrill fit in?'

'I think Cherrill is the boil on Shawcross's backside. Maybe he thinks that he should siphon off some of the consortium's profits or maybe he has a grudge. I don't know.'

'It's getting more interesting by the minute. I'll tell you straight, Tottie, I want Ramsey.'

'Oh? Something personal?'

'Yeh, and I don't want to talk about it.'

'It's your show...' Suddenly he pulled up and was off his mount and kneeling on the ground and examining a horse apple. He looked up and grinned at Tumbleweed.

'We're on the right track. They cut across the trail a while back and this isn't more than four hours old. They've been travelling all night and they're moving slow. Those horses are tired and need feed. Look, there's blood spots on those stones. One of them is injured and it looks as if there's a lame horse with them.'

Tumbleweed looked and he marvelled how Tottie read the ground like a book. The signs were all there when they were pointed out to him. No wonder Tottie was relaxed and just waiting for the right time to connect. He smiled.

'So you think the lame horse and the

injured party will slow up the gang?'

'Could be. That'll be why we've caught up so quickly. But they'll be getting impatient. They'll want to move on fast...'

Suddenly there were the faint sounds of gunshots coming from over the brow of the hill. Both men reacted at once. Tumbleweed spurred his horse forward and Tottie leapt aboard and was pounding after him.

They pulled up at the crest of a rise and watched the scene down below in the valley. There was a small cabin with smoke rising from its chimney. As they watched, a puff of smoke and a gunshot echoed around the distant hills. Someone was firing from inside. Tumbleweed's eyes raked the wooded undergrowth on the valley floor and saw movement. Two shots came and the bullets embedded themselves in the log wall. Then a window shattered and Tumbleweed reckoned it was time to interfere.

'Right. You take the one on the left and I'll concentrate on the right. There were four of them, so there's two to watch for.'

'Then there was the woman and the boy.'

'Hm, I'd forgotten them. Yeh, just mind what you're doing. I wonder if Mort and young Drydon have heard the racket?'

'Old Mort's no fool and won't run into

trouble easy. He'll hold back and come in at the right time. I know old Mort, a regular pro.'

'Then let's get to it.' And with that they tethered the horses and slipped over the ridge to snake down from one bit of ground cover to the next.

It was Tottie who scored first. Tumbleweed could hear his gun blazing away. It caused the second man to break cover and Tumbleweed's bullet caught him between the shoulder-blades. His arms spread wide and he leapt into the air only to come down like a rag doll with the stuffing gone.

Tumbleweed looked about him for signs of the others. Then he heard the pounding of horses' feet and knew that whoever they were were too far ahead for them to be caught. Cursing, he turned towards where he had seen Tottie running. He found him bent over a crumbled figure. He rose as Tumbleweed came up. He looked grim.

'He's dead, but he talked before he died.'

'Oh, did he want to?'

'Nope. But he was persuaded.' He gave a wintry smile, and Tumbleweed shivered. There was a lot of Indian in Tottie.

'What's been happening here?'

'The cabin's abandoned. They stopped to

rest and feed the horses. It seems that the girl and the kid have been holding them back. There was an argument between the other four. Cherrill wanted them killed and one of them objected. The girl overheard and barricaded the cabin and wouldn't let them in. The kid's laid up inside with a bullet wound got when they left town. The girl's nag's lamed and that's the situation. Do we go and see what's happening down there or go on after Cherrill? He'll be sticking to that bank roll like shit to a blanket.'

'We'll follow later. He knows we're close after him and will be holing up somewhere to bushwhack us. We'll let him sweat it out and we'll go see what we can do for the woman.'

'She might take a potshot at us.'

'We'll go in from the back. We'll circle round. Anyway, I'm not after her,' – Tottie gave a sly grin which Tumbleweed studiously ignored, – 'I'm after bigger fish!'

The woman was bending over a bed made of cedar branches when Tumbleweed kicked the door open. She rose sharply and a Colt much too heavy for her wavered in her hand.

'Stand right there, mister, or I'll shoot you in the bollocks!'

There was a wild look about her and

Tumbleweed was aware how nervous trigger fingers could act up funny and he didn't want to go through life as a eunuch. He froze and prayed that Tottie would make it fast.

'Take it easy, lady. I've just shot one of those bastards who was shooting at you.' The pistol wavered.

'Get your hands up and keep 'em up. How do I know you're not one of the men Cherrill was expecting?'

Tumbleweed looked puzzled.

'He was meeting someone here?'

'Yeh, he mentioned a pay-off but changed his mind. One of Shawcross's minders was going to collect. That was what keeps Cherrill in business,' she finished bitterly. 'He decided to move on so figured he didn't need pay out. He was going to leave Shaw-cross flat. The bastard deserved it anyway. It's what he's done to me and my kid brother here that's got my back up. I'll get the bastard if it's the last thing I do!'

'Well, I assure you I'm not here to collect.'

'No, but I am!' Old Mort stepped from behind the open door, the business end of his old Navy Colt staring at Tumbleweed in the belly. 'I have no quarrel with you, mister, so step aside and you, miss, put that thing down before you shoot yourself in the foot.'

She glanced at the boy on the bed and then seeing the situation was hopeless she dropped the weapon but within reach if need arose.

'Well, what do you want now, Mort?' Tumbleweed relaxed a little for he'd seen the shadow of movement at the window.

'It's time we all put our cards on the table...' Mort stopped abruptly as a crashing body dived through the window in a tight ball and come up waving a gun.

'It's OK, Tottie, you can relax. Old Mort here is just going to explain something.'

Tottie dusted splinters of glass from his person. His face was cut and blood dribbled and he cursed mildly.

'You might have warned me,' he grumbled. 'I might have sliced my head off! Now what's this all about?'

Mort looked about him and laughed mirthlessly.

'We've all been had. Me, because I was supposed to be taking Hawkins' cut from the raid. It was to be shared between him and Shawcross and I was to get a cut from Hawkins. You,' – turning to Tumbleweed, – 'because it showed the townsfolk that he was willing to send a posse after Cherrill, and Tottie because it was natural that he

41

should send the best tracker with you.'

'What about the youngster, Drydon?'

'Ah, now he was different. He knows nothing. He came because I got Hawkins to choose him. I leant on Hawkins...' He chuckled. 'I know things about Hawkins he wouldn't like his neighbours to know.'

'But why Drydon? Where the hell is he, anyway?'

'Up that hill yonder looking after the horses. I didn't want him getting hurt!'

'Jesus Christ! Why bring him along if you don't want him hurt?'

The old man looked sly.

'Ah, now we come to it. I wasn't going back with that cash if Cherrill had honoured the arrangement. I was lighting out and as the youngster is my pard, he was going with me. I was going to set the kid up in a small ranch well away from these parts and then I was going to sit me down for the rest of my natural and take it easy. Anything wrong in that?'

Tumbleweed grinned. 'Not from where I stand. I suppose the idea is still good?'

'Yeh, but the cash is missing.'

'With a bit of effort and co-operation we might get the whole boodle. What do you think Shawcross would think of that?'

Mort's eyes gleamed and he slowly looked around at them all.

'You all feel like that?'

The woman was watching and listening open-mouthed. Tottie was impassive as usual but he licked his lips. Tumbleweed grinned inside. They were all taken with the idea. It was easy to manipulate people when cash was involved. Now he looked at the woman.

'How about you, ma'am? You don't seem to have had a fair deal from Cherrill?'

'You can say that again, mister! I don't know about this Shawcross guy, but I'm sure going after Cherrill. He promised to marry me and make me a lady! He got me into this on that promise, then the bastard was ready to have me killed because my brother was slowing them down and I suppose I knew too much!'

Just then there was a groan from the bed and she bent over the youth lying so still.

'Carlos, can you hear me?' She wetted his lips with water from a bowl by the bed. Carlos did not respond. She looked at Tumbleweed.

'There's a bullet in his shoulder. Could you dig it out?'

'Yeh, I've dug a few Yankie bullets out in my time. It'll have to be done or else lead poison'll kill him. Tottie, you can help.'

'No, you get a fire going, Tottie. I'll help this feller here.' Mort elbowed Tottie away. He looked at the woman. 'And you, missie, if you've any food in your saddle-bags make us some grub and brew some coffee. I'm an old man and I need food. I don't know about you lot but I cain't traipse all over the country on an empty belly. What's your name, miss? We might as well all be friendly like.'

'Maria, Maria Sanchez and my brother is Carlos. We live in Mexico. That's where I met Lee Cherrill and I thought I was his woman. He used me...' Her voice faltered. 'He said he would make Carlos a rich man and then he could buy plenty of cattle and build up my grandfather's ranch.'

Tumbleweed pricked up his ears. So Maria had met Cherill on a ranch, which might be the gang's hole-up. He would ask Maria about it later, for now he was tearing away the bloody shirt that covered the boy's wound. It looked bad. It was already festering.

The boy moaned at the treatment. Tumbleweed was as gentle as he was able. He gestured to Mort.

'Got that whiskey bottle handy?'

44

Mort drew it from his hip pocket a little reluctantly.

'Just wet his lips, eh? No need to waste the stuff. He might cock his toes!'

Tumbleweed took it, giving Mort a look of contempt. 'Don't be a bastard, Mort. Someday you might want someone to give you a drink when you most need it.'

Mort managed to look ashamed. 'It's the only bottle I have,' he mumbled, 'but the kid's welcome to a smidgeon.'

The dry sticks Tottie collected were soon well alight and an old black stewpan filled with water was soon boiled for coffee. Tumbleweed sterilised his knife in the flames and set about the task of digging out the bullet after giving Carlos a practised crack on the jaw, just hard enough to knock him out but not break his jaw.

He swabbed the raw gaping hole with Mort's whiskey which brought Carlos round fast. He screamed. Tumbleweed rammed the handle of his gun into Carlo's mouth. Carlos bit hard and the scream ceased.

'I want a bandage. Maria, what you wearing under that blouse?'

For a moment Maria looked outraged and then she understood. She turned her back and pulled her blouse over her head showing a white cotton bodice. This she slipped off after undoing the front buttons. Tumbleweed watched as her honey-gold back was revealed. Again he felt her attraction but this was no time to allow feelings to erupt.

She thrust the garment into his outstretched hand. For an instant he could smell the scent of her body, then he was tearing the bodice into wide strips.

Mort, holding the boy's shaking body, watched silently as Tumbleweed bound the wound. It was a rough and ready operation. Tumbleweed was no surgeon and his hands held no tenderness. He leaned back, sweat dripping from his brow.

'There, I've done all I can. He's young. He'll get over the ordeal. What about another shot of Mort's whiskey?'

Mort eyed Tumbleweed with disgust but silently offered what was left in the bottle. Carlos took a small snort, choked and pushed the bottle away. Mort inspected what was left and promptly emptied the bottle in one swallow, then belched.

Coffee was now brewing and Maria fried salted belly pork and made corn flapjacks with cornmeal from her saddle-bag. They ate swiftly and after the meal Tumbleweed came to a decision.

'Maria, can you think of a good hideout to take your brother? We've got to get you away from here. I have a feeling the sheriff will come looking for his cut.'

'How can we move him? He'll never fork a horse.'

'I was thinking about that. Mort, what about sending young Drydon back to find the old potman?'

Mort stared at Tumbleweed as if he'd gone mad.

'You can't send that kid back! The townsfolk would have his guts for sausage skins! If they get an inkling of what's going on then all hell would break loose!'

'I'll go,' said Indian Tottie. 'I want to see Bet, anyway. I have a feeling that Hawkins is sniffing her petticoats. If I catch 'em...' His voice tailed away but everyone was aware of the violence smouldering just under the surface.

Tumbleweed spoke sharply. 'Whatever you find, Tottie, it can wait. We don't want you advertising your presence. You'll go in and out of that town like one of your nature spirits. You might even catch the old drummer on his way out of town.'

Tottie shrugged. 'I'll not go in. I'll make my way to Molly's place and get word to Bet

47

and she can tell the oldster to bring the wagon to my place.' He scowled at Tumbleweed. 'Folk will think Bet's after tumbling him.' He waited for Tumbleweed to make some adverse comment but Tumbleweed kept any thoughts he had on the subject of Bet to himself. It was of no concern to him what Bet did or didn't do. He couldn't quite fathom Tottie's way of thinking however. He was aware of Bet's failing and yet lived with it, and yet was ready to kill Hawkins if he found him with her. It was incomprehensible.

He shrugged. 'I don't care how you do it, but get him here as fast as is possible; by midnight or just after. Then you,' – turning to Maria – 'can take your brother to the nearest safe hiding place.'

'Not so fast, mister. You're not giving me orders! The old man can take Carlos back to our grandfather. I'm riding with you!'

'Like hell you are!'

'I have the right! If you knew how Lee Cherrill used me, then you wouldn't stop me!' Wild of eye and bosom heaving, she challenged him. She stood with legs apart, hands on hips and even through the now soiled blouse he was aware of her sexuality.

He didn't want her with them for the truth

of the matter was that she threatened his concentration. Going after Lee Cherrill was only another step in getting nearer to Ted Ramsey.

'Look, isn't your first duty to your brother? I'll get Cherill, never fear. Doesn't that satisfy you?'

'No! I want to see the bastard killed and I want to be part of it! You won't shift me on this, mister. If you won't take me, I'll follow behind and damn you to hell!'

He nodded. He recognized a determined, reckless female when he came up against one. She would rather ride through fire than change her mind and he gave up the contest. He sighed. It was going to be hell trying to think of her as a feller!

'If you ride with us you'll have to get rid of that ridiculous blouse. You'll be a feller and we'll treat you like one,' he grunted.

She smiled triumphantly.

'Don't worry; I'm tough. I was brought up to ride all day on my grandfather's ranch. I can throw a steer with the best. Does that satisfy you?'

'Huh! Maybe. How are you with a rifle?'

'Do you want to come outside and I'll show you?'

Tumbleweed looked at her with grudging respect, seeing beyond the outward charms.

She was no shrinking violet and had knocked around and given herself for either love or money, and yet there was a passion and loyalty waiting for the right man and that man would surely be the luckiest bastard in the whole wild world. He smiled, and it changed his entire face. She smiled back.

'Thank you. I appreciate you're going against your better judgement. I promise I'll not be a drag on you.' She spoke quietly, now released from all emotion. 'Have you a shirt I can wear?'

Silently he went outside to his saddle-bag and brought back his only clean shirt. He handed it to her with a reluctant grin.

'It's the only one I've got. We're going to smell mighty bad before we tote Cherrill back to San Paulo!'

THREE

It was two days before they were ready to start. The trail would be growing cold but the Indian, Tottie did not appear worried. He could follow Indian spoor across rocks, so following two men on horseback was no problem. Besides, it would give Cherrill a feeling of security when he stopped to look back and saw no tell-tale puff of dust following him.

After Tottie had returned with the drummer who was known as Pig Whistle because of his smell, young Carlos had taken a turn for the worse. He was delirious for most of the time and Tumbleweed, reluctantly, had decided that the septic wound must be cauterized.

This was done with the minimum of fuss. Pig Whistle forced whiskey down the boy's throat and Mort and a green-faced Drydon held him down. Tottie blew on the embers of the fire and heated his own Bowie knife until the broad blade was shining red. Then he handed it to Tumbleweed carefully as the heat scorched both their faces. The two men gave each other one long, meaningful look and then Tottie nodded.

'It's the only way.' Tumbleweed plunged the knife into the festering wound and turned it swiftly. There was the stench of burning flesh, and Maria, banished outside the cabin, retched and threw up.

Carlos screamed and arched his back while the old man and the youth strained to hold him down. Tottie caught his thrashing

51

legs and laid his full weight on him. Then the boy fainted.

Tumbleweed threw down the still red-hot knife on to the hearth.

'See to him,' he said, and stumbled outside. He found Maria on her knees. He went to her without a word and drew her up so that her head was on his chest. The woman smell of her tickled his nostrils but at this time it meant nothing. They clung together gathering strength from each other. For both it had been a trauma.

Then she stirred. 'Will he be all right?'

He could feel the tension in her as she waited for his reply. He massaged her back to relieve the knots.

'Yes. He'll have a nasty scar and a stiff shoulder but he'll be fine. I'm sorry he screamed. I'm not a surgeon and I've never fired a wound before.'

He felt her shiver.

'Poor Carlos, he's only sixteen. I'll never forgive myself. He came because I wanted his help for Lee. I told him Lee could make his fortune and now it has come to this! Oh, how I hate that man!'

'What's done is done. It's all in the past. Carlos will be fine, you'll see.'

Again she clung to him, overcome by a

trembling she couldn't control and all he could do was hold her close until the storm abated.

He thought of that brief moment as they set out at dawn of the next day. It was grey ghost time and the wind blew cold. Pig Whistle had agreed to delay their departure for another day until Carlos was somewhat recovered. Maria's farewell to her brother had been emotional. Now she was quiet and subdued as she and Tumbleweed followed Tottie, with Mort and Drydon following behind them.

For a while it looked as if the two horsemen had covered their tracks. Tottie went ahead and circled while the others moved slowly ahead to save their horses. Then Tottie could be seen to the far left across the plain. He was waving and his voice came faint on the breeze.

'It looks as if he's cut sign,' Tumbleweed shouted to the two men behind him and they rowelled their horses and thundered to meet him. Tumbleweed gave Maria a sideways glance. She looked like a boy in her denims and brown checked shirt too big for her and an old broad-brimmed black hat found in Pig Whistle's wagon holding up her long black hair. She looked very different to the undulating dancer he'd seen on Main Street in San Paulo. She also rode like a man which was all that mattered at this time.

There was a pistol at her narrow waist, half-hidden by Carlo's bloody jerkin which she'd sponged but couldn't hide the bullet hole at the shoulder. It gave her the air of a desperado. She looked like a fresh-faced Billy the Kid.

They drew up in a welter of dust. Tottie was grinning, unusual for him.

'The cunning bastards thought they'd covered their tracks by wading down-stream before riding on. I had a hunch about that stream as soon as I saw it.'

Tottie was covered in dry mud splashes and his horse lathered. He'd returned fast after locating the entry and exit of the fugitives. It would now be painstaking search and watch; to be done slowly and deliberately to let them lead the way to their hideout.

They stopped to eat and fodder the horses for they were of prime concern. No good wearing out good horses. A man's life depended on how good was the horse under him.

They ate better than they would have done without Maria. She insisted on rustling up panbread and had brought long strips of beef already cooked the day before.

Young Drydon was already her slave and fetched wood for the fire and for the first time seemed to enjoy the manhunt. Mort, however, still grumbled and repeatedly cursed Cherrill for double-crossing them, until Tumbleweed told him sharply to shut his mouth or he would shut it for him.

Tottie sat alone and ate his food, staring into the distance. No one cared to disturb him.

Maria rested. Her body ached for it had been quite some time since she had spent so many hours in the saddle. But she would have never admitted this to Tumbleweed. She would rather die over a slow fire than admit to this man that she might have been wrong in thinking that she could keep up with them.

The sun was casting shadows when Tumbleweed stood up and stretched. Tottie was on his feet in an instant. Young Drydon still snored by the side of old Mort, replete and sluggish.

Tumbleweed stared down at the pair. What the hell was he doing with these two? If anyone was to crack up he'd bet money on either of these two before Maria. However he had no choice. He wouldn't give them a snowball in hell's chance if they went back to face Hawkins.

He kicked them both sharply in the ribs.

'Time to go, fellers. Get your rigs and we'll be away.'

Drydon groaned. 'Jesus! I'm stiff,' he moaned. 'It doesn't seem five minutes...'

Mort stumbled to his feet.

'Quit squawking, kid. You've got a full belly and we've got a long ride out yet! You don't know what it means to really suffer!'

'Aw, hell, Mort, I was only saying...'

'Then don't. The boss don't like it by half.'

The kid moodily packed their gear and was ready to ride when Maria came back from behind a bush having done what was needful. They followed in the same order as previously, but now Maria had stripped off her jerkin and Tumbleweed was conscious of thrusting breasts and swelling womanly hips.

It was an uncomfortable ride for Tumbleweed and he cursed under his breath. He was a red-blooded male and the little lady didn't realize just what she was putting him through, or did she? He found himself remembering the coolly confident way he'd told her that she would be treated as a man. Like hell he could! He might pretend he would treat her like a man but at the end of the day she was still all woman...

They paddled their way downstream and came out at the same spot where the mud was churned up by the other horses. Tottie reckoned they were no more than six hours behind their quarries. Pushing on, they rode well into the darkness before finding a place to rest the horses.

They made cold camp for now a fire might be seen at a great distance in this flat valley country especially if someone was looking back for an indication of pursuit.

Tumbleweed took first watch for he was uneasy and not just for what lay ahead. His body twitched and was sending out messages his mind couldn't give in to, not if he wanted to keep that woman's respect.

Thoughts of Ted Ramsey came to torment him. These days his young wife's face was only a blur, but the scene that had confronted him when he'd returned home to his parents' ranch was as clear now as it was the day it happened.

It should have been a good day. It was time of harvest and they had all been out in the fields when Quantrill's wild mob had ridden in. Now the war between the States was over, the bunch had openly turned outlaw. They needed the excitement of fighting. None of them could or wanted to return to the humdrum life of ranchers and farmers. They needed the smell of blood.

He'd often wondered whether the outcome would have been different if he'd come home a day earlier. At least the rape of his wife and the ultimate shooting down of the prisoners would not have happened so tamely. Some of those sons of the devil would never have seen another sunrise. He'd wanted to die along with his folks. Instead, he'd buried them and a hard knot of hate grew inside him and it burned and burned...

Now he found it still burned with the old fire when he thought of Ramsey and how he was now nearer to him than at any time in the last six years. Revenge was going to be sweet...

A movement, and Tumbleweed reacted automatically and his Colt glinted in the moonlight. He lowered the weapon when Maria moved out of the shadow.

'What the hell? You shouldn't do that,' he reproved. 'One of these days you might get killed.'

'I couldn't sleep. Too much on my mind. Can we talk?'

'Yeh, If you must, but you should be resting. The next few days will tax all of us.'

'I'll manage,' she said briefly. 'What I want you to know is that I'm not just a common whore. I loved Lee Cherrill. I gave him everything a girl dreams of giving. Understand? I believed in his love for me and I believed every word he said.' She stopped, and her eyes stared into a distance Tumbleweed couldn't share. 'I should have listened to Grandfather. He never liked him even though he brought him bunches of steers to build up the herd we'd lost. There were three drought years on the trot and we were about to abandon the ranch...'

'And Cherrill came along and it was his way of bribing your grandfather to turn the ranch into a hideout. I bet it was high in the mountains, secluded, and not far over the border?'

'Yes; how did you guess?'

Tumbleweed shrugged. 'It figures. That's how Quantrill worked. If folk didn't co-operate he burned them out and left no one to talk. Ted Ramsey did the same and when Cherrill joined the gang he would have learned all the tricks. You were a bonus. Wrap you round his little finger and he could get your grandfather to do everything he wanted, and he wouldn't dare tell you if he was threatened. I bet the bastard threatened to

59

kill you if the old man talked.'

Maria looked stunned. 'I never realized ... even now I've only thought of myself and the way he's treated me and Carlos! I never thought of how Grandfather would feel when both Carlos and myself rode away with Lee and his bunch! And it was I who persuaded Carlos to come with us. Lee thought he was too young. I insisted, thinking that Lee would show him how to make a fortune!'

'You were very innocent, Maria. How long's it been?'

'Going on two years.'

'And were they happy years?'

Maria hung her head.

'No. At first it was an adventure. I'd seen nothing, gone nowhere, and it was all so new and exciting. We used to go home when things got too hot and Lee gave Grandfather money and sometimes some prize cattle. Said he was building up a good herd for the future. I thought we should settle down on the ranch and help Grandfather eventually.'

'What about Carlos?'

'Oh, he never wanted to stay at the ranch. A few days and he wanted to be away. It was too slow for him, he said. He liked Lee. He told him wonderful tales of adventure and fighting Indians and getting the pick of the best women…' She bit her lip. 'Sometimes I hated him when he talked like that. This last raid was going to be his last, so he said. There was something special about it. There was to be more cash than usual in the safe and Lee said there was some double-crossing going on and he was going to have his cut and we had to be ready to run.'

'And then you found out the hard way that he was going to cut and run without you. That's about the size of it, isn't it?'

She nodded her head. 'God, how I hate him! Don't you dare kill him! I want him.'

'And what then!'

Maria looked about her, her hands balled into fists and then she turned and looked at Tumbleweed full in the face.

'I'll do what the Indians do; put him over a slow fire and cut off his pecker and ram it down his throat!'

Tumbleweed coughed. The thought brought tears to his eyes. She was angry enough and passionate enough to do just that. He pitied Lee Cherrill, if ever Maria caught up with him.

'Revenge is never sweet,' he found himself muttering and then he wondered why he said that. It would be sweet when he caught

61

up with Ramsey. Maybe it was because he didn't like the idea of Maria having such thoughts.

'I don't care if it's sweet or not. It's what's going to happen! No one is going to make a fool of Maria Sanchez! Not and live to talk about it!'

'It'll eat into you, Maria. It'll make you ill, like a canker. Women aren't built for revenge. I'm going to take his body back to San Paulo and that's all there is to it.'

'Then it will be a matter of who gets at him first!'

'Maria, go to bed and quieten your mind and sleep. It will be a big day tomorrow.'

Suddenly, Maria's mood changed. She smiled at him as if just aware of him.

'Maybe you could quieten me down as you put it. What d'you say?'

He stared down at her face inches below his own. She was warm and tantalizing and deliberately...

'You're actually asking me...?'

'Yes, why not? I know you want me. Wouldn't any man?' She put out a hand and stroked his bristly cheek. He felt the thrill of her caress under his skin and it shot waves of pleasure to his groin. His breath came in a huge gust. She smiled triumphantly.

'Come on, we both want it ... what are you waiting for?'

It was the hardest thing in the world to push her away, but he knew, once he had tasted that delectable flesh he would never be his own man again.

'You forgot, on this trip I'm treating you as a man!'

She drew back, temper shooting sparks from her eyes.

'You bastard! You encouraged me!' She raised her fist to strike him. He caught her wrist and twisted it cruelly up her back.

'You encouraged yourself. You wanted me like an animal wants a mate and I don't play the stud for any woman. I do the choosing, the time and the place. Now get yourself back to bed or go throw cold water over yourself!'

They did not speak as they plodded their way behind Tottie. The sun was hot on their backs and their shirts clung to them with darkened patches of sweat. For a time Maria held back and rode with Drydon but Mort came between them and as Mort's smell was on the rise she quickly moved ahead alongside Tumbleweed again. Since breakfast she had pointedly ignored him. Now she was sick of her own thoughts.

She forgot everything as they drew up to Tottie who was waiting for them at the crest of the last long slope they'd wearily ridden. Tottie stretched out a hand to the rolling scene ahead.

'They're somewhere down there, I reckon. This is good hideout country. I figure it might be an idea for you to rest up and I'll scout ahead and see if I can get another lead. The trail is getting harder to follow. We're coming to hard ground.'

'There's no need,' Maria said softly. 'I know exactly where we are.' She pointed excitedly to a pinnacle of rock reaching high into the air far down below. 'That's Moon Woman's Needle. Lee uses it as a guide to his hideout in these parts. You would never find it if you didn't know where to look. There's a split in the range on the far side of the valley, a kind of gorge where a river flows. You have to walk up river. That's why no one can follow the trail.'

'Does he have guards?'

'No. He thinks he's too well hidden. Besides, I've never known more than six members of his gang, sometimes less. Lee was never one to let too many into his confidence. That would be why he wanted

Carlos and I dead.' The bitterness in her was like acid.

'So he won't expect us?'

'No. He'll have watched his backtrail and he'll think he's in the clear.'

'Good. Then if Tottie scouts ahead, we might just get in and give him and whoever's with him a surprise. How many men with him do you reckon, Maria?'

'I think it would be Hal Clausen riding with him. He's got ginger hair. Unless you shot him?'

Tumbleweed shook his head. 'The ones we shot were black-haired.'

'Then it would be Clausen. He's a dangerous bastard and cool. There would be the old Mex who looks after the place and his son who looks after the horses and any cattle they bring in. And there's Joe Mayrick who got shot in the thigh and missed the raid. That's all.'

'So we have a good chance of surprise.'

'More so if Lee does as he usually does. He celebrates his success and Joe and Hal are always enthusiastic drinkers!'

'Better still. That bank roll will be a good reason to crack a bottle or two.'

Maria looked pensive.

'I'm not so sure this time. I don't think

Lee means to share out. It was to be his last fling in these parts. I think he might hide the cash and go in with his tail between his legs as if he'd failed.'

'But what about Hal? He would know; unless he made up some tale about sharing just with Hal...'

Maria bit her lip.

'I don't like to say this, but Hal could be in big trouble. So could the others. Just think, they're the only ones who know about the hideout. It stands to reason he's not going to leave them alive!'

'Maybe it's a good thing you're with us, Maria. If he gets away, he's going to go after Carlos and yourself. He knows you're both still alive.'

'But he's not going to get away, is he?' And Maria's reckless laugh echoed down the valley.

Tottie dismounted and led his horse to a patch of green and tethered him. His glance at Maria was unfathomable. Tumbleweed could never decide whether Tottie approved of her or not.

'We'll camp in the trees,' he murmured softly to Tumbleweed. 'I don't trust old Mort or that young Drydon not to do something foolish. I'm going to eat fast and then I'm going to take a looksee. Keep that woman quiet. Her laughter could be heard for miles. If I'm not back in three hours then take a warning and come on slow and careful.'

Tumbleweed nodded. 'Any ideas about moving in? I still don't think Maria's figuring about no guards is the right one. It takes a mighty confident leader to do away with guards, especially when he's just robbed the big boss. What d'you think?'

'Yeh, I'd think twice about what that woman says. She might hate Cherrill and talk about killing him, but when it comes to make-up-your-mind time, maybe it's all bunkum, especially when you refused to sleep with her!'

Tumbleweed was astonished and Tottie grinned at his expression.

'Well, y'bugger...' Tumbleweed choked and spluttered.

'Sorry, boss, but I sleep light. Nobody stirs around me but I'm awake. I'm sorry.'

'So you should be! Well, forget it. It's no business of yours!'

Tottie hunched his shoulders. 'Maybe not. But we all know there's something wrong between you. Even Drydon who don't usually see an inch before his face knows something's up; but you're the boss. But if I were you, I'd do something about it. Women are funny creatures!'

Tottie loped off with his lithe energy-saving movements to fill his belly and be on his way. Tumbleweed envied him. His own lower spine ached from an old injury sustained on a round-up of wild horses back in Montana. He'd got entangled in a running rope and was clean yanked out of the saddle. He moved and stretched. He could sure use the time Tottie would be away to iron out the kinks.

Drydon ran a rope between two young cottonwoods for tethering the horses. He foddered his own and left it with the others in line after feeding it with a handful of oats from the sack in his saddle-bags and running his hand down all four legs to check for lameness. Watering would come later.

Old Mort had a fire going and already there was a pungent smell of coffee brewing. Maria fussed around doing the fixin's and after the chow was wolfed down he moved away to clean his guns and ease his aching back.

He saw Maria silently watching him. Maybe Tottie was right and he should make an effort to put things right.

'Give me your gun and I'll clean it. How

much ammunition have you got?'

'Enough.' The answer was terse but she dropped the gun within reach.

Hands busy, he did not look at her as he worked on the weapon and spoke softly, 'It's not what you think, Maria. I want you very much. But not like an animal. If you'd made me that offer back in town and we'd had time to get to know each other, then things would have been different. Understand what I mean?'

'I understand you refused a good thing!'

Tumbleweed sighed. She was still as mad as fire.

'I'm not in the habit of asking for it! In fact, the only other men I've slept with were because of Lee Cherrill! He was that kind of man, and I loved him so much I went along with it! Do *you* understand that?'

Tumbleweed looked at her with pity and something in his eyes made her turn away.

'So you've never slept with anyone who really loved you?'

Swiftly she turned back to him, eyes bright with unshed tears and temper.

'I thought he loved me! I think all you men are bastards! You're all out to exploit women. My own poor mother ... oh, hell, what's the use of talking about it! It's over.' She turned away and Tumbleweed could see by the set of her shoulders that she was still angry.

'Maria, I'm sorry. I was a clumsy fool.'

'Yes, so you were.'

'Can we be friends again? We have a common aim...'

She bent over him. He could smell the elusive scent of her. It reminded him bitterly what he had refused. He'd been a fool...

'Just remember that, mister. We've only one thing in common ... Lee Cherrill!'

Wordlessly he looked at her and handed back her gun.

Tottie returned as quietly as he'd left. The sun was low and casting shadows. He sank down beside Tumbleweed and reached for one of the black cigarillos he loved.

Tumbleweed waited patiently. Tottie wouldn't answer questions until he was good and ready. Drawing luxuriously on the cigarillo as if he hadn't smoked for a long time, he looked at Tumbleweed and grinned.

'The woman was right. There's no guards. The place is wide open. I can't understand the guy. There's an old Mex and a man who might be his son. They were around doing chores. They'll be no danger. In fact I think the place belongs to the younger man. I saw Cherrill come out of the cabin to piss. I

70

managed to get near enough to have a looksee into the cabin. It was dark but the man who rode with Cherrill was talking to another man...'

'Some feller who got shot up.'

'Oh, that accounts for him not coming out. I watched for a long time and then the second man came out and bawled for the old Mex. He wanted him to look the horses over. Evidently the Mex shoes horses. He also mentioned a mule. It looks as if he and Cherrill are riding out and planning a long journey.' He grinned again. 'I wonder if that feller expects to share Cherrill's loot?'

'Maria doesn't think he'll share with anyone. I think he's planning a whole new life. He's going to get a mighty surprise. When do you reckon will be the best time to move in?'

'Do as the Indians do, an hour before dawn before they're awake and reckoning. Confuse 'em and get it over, quick.'

'Right. We'll move out after dark and get settled in to wait. We'll fodder the horses well now and water them and then they won't be bloated when we need 'em most.'

'I'll go and rake out the others and see if that woman has saved me something to eat. Man, I'm starved!'

The journey was made in silence. Sticking to the deep shadows and picking their way behind Tottie, they made their way to the Moon Woman's Needle. Silently Tottie pointed in the direction in which to go and headed for another butte that loomed up in the darkness. They headed that way and the ground was now turning arid and infertile but Tottie carried on. Tumbleweed was having doubts.

'Are you sure you're on the right track?' he whispered to Tottie.

Tottie turned in the saddle and gave Tumbleweed a filthy look, and didn't even bother to answer. He looked back to try and figure Maria's expression. She would know if Tottie was making a mistake, but Maria rode with Drydon on one side of her and old Mort on the other and she held her head down as if tired.

Then Tottie was sliding off his horse and they all stopped.

'From now on we walk the horses and we nip their noses in case one of them panics. One whinny and it'll set 'em all off and I wouldn't guarantee us getting through the pass. It could be a death-trap if it was guarded.'

Tumbleweed nodded and pulled his horse

round and went back to explain the situation to the others.

'I don't like it,' complained the youth. 'It sounds like we could be sitting ducks!'

'You don't have to go any further, buster. You can stay on the outside. Mind you, there's no guarantee there's no one up there, in those rocks watching us right at this moment. You can take your choice.'

Young Drydon shivered. 'I wish to God I'd never come along. I'm no fighter. If it hadn't been old Mort...'

'Aw, shaddup and stop whining! Maria, you know what to expect?'

'Of course. I've been through that ravine several times. It's just a cut through rock, like a dry river bed. An hour's walking and we'll be through it.' She looked with contempt at Drydon. 'What a pity a nice-looking boy like you has no balls!'

The youth flushed, and his Adam's apple popped up and down like a cork in water.

Old Mort stamped around. He listened in silence to what had been said. Now he turned on both Maria and Drydon.

'There's no call for you to be rude, ma'am. The kid's had no real experience of violence. I've always looked after him...'

'More fool you! He's that green, you'll get

him killed. It's time he squared up to the real world!'

Mort was now in a fine old rage.

'He's a good kid and I'll not let the likes of you who's nothing but an outlaw's whore call him names!'

Maria lunged forward and smacked the old man on the jaw before anyone could stop her.

'You dirty old pig! All you want is to suck on to the kid. You think you've got it made for the rest of your rotten life! But I tell you, once he finds himself a woman, he'll leave you flat ... if he lives long enough!'

Mort wiped his mouth, hand shaking. Words hovered on his lips and then he turned away, eyes lighting on Drydon. His fury turned on him.

'What you staring at? And what's this fool talk about staying behind? Of course you're coming with us, or are you the weak yellow-livered coward she says you are?'

Drydon turned away, head down. 'I'm coming with you. I never said I wasn't.'

'Good. Then no more complaining or as old as I am I'll whup your arse good and proper.'

Tottie, listening to the argument, frowned. For a small party they were a mixed up

74

bunch. He wished Hawkins hadn't thought it necessary to send Mort and the boy with them to make it look good for the townsfolk. Damn the sheriff! He could depend on the woman's hate to see her through but he was damned if the boy and the old man would be an asset to them. Still, he could send them on ahead. All they had to do was follow their noses. If Cherrill had put a guard on the opening into the next valley, then those two bozos were the ones deserving of the pot-shots.

He motioned to Drydon.

'Get moving and we'll follow behind.'

Mort lifted his head sharply. 'What do you mean letting the boy go first?'

'You heard. You cover him if you want. We follow behind.' And suddenly Tottie's Colt was aiming at Mort's stomach. The old man stared.

'Tottie, we've known each other for years...' He licked his lips.

'And you always were an awkward old coot, and I haven't forgotten some of the names you called me and my ma. Now get moving, both of you!'

Slowly they moved forward, horses on close rein. Both horses were twitchy, neither beast used to leading, and it was a struggle to make them move forward into the darkness of the narrow gorge.

The walls rose sheer and in daylight they would have seen age-old signs of water cutting through rock. But now the sandy bed of river was just a winding boulder-strewn trail that was difficult to manoeuvre. The horses picked their way slowly, often stumbling and fighting to free themselves from strong, firm hands.

Tumbleweed saw Maria being dragged by her mare, making his own horse leap and quiver and so he motioned for her to hold her mare's nose while he took the reins and walked between both animals.

As they walked, the moon came up and there was a slither of indigo sky up above and when the clouds rolled away there was a little moonlight to make their way easier.

They were nearing the end of the gorge and Drydon was now walking with more confidence. No one or nothing stirred, not even a night owl. He could see the path widening and before Tumbleweed realized his intention, the boy forked his horse and was preparing to ride out into the hidden valley in full moonlight.

Tumbleweed shouted, but too late; a shot rang out and Drydon flung up his hands as the horse reared and the boy's body crashed to the ground with a dull thud.

Old Mort yelled, his horse rearing, and he struggled to reach the boy he regarded as a son as Tumbleweed raked the shadowed side of the cliffs for movement. A thin puff of smoke could be sensed rather than seen. He risked a wild shot but there was no answering yell. Whoever had shot Drydon had moved quickly.

Cursing, Tumbleweed yelled to Mort. 'Get back into cover, you old fool!' But Mort was not listening. He was struggling to lift the boy in his arms, tears rolling down his withered old cheeks.

'The bastard's killed him,' he croaked. 'God damn him to hell! He never had a chance.'

'Leave him, Mort, we'll pick him up later. You can't help him now.'

Old Mort erupted in fury.

'The devils! I'll have Cherrill's guts...' He allowed the body to fall and rushed out into the open space near the valley entrance. Again came the whining of a rifle bullet. Mort spun round and dropped, hands clawing at the earth but this time Tumbleweed was ready and aimed for the tell-tale sign of rifle fire.

A scream, and a body hurtled down from an underlying crag. It was Hal Clausen, shot in the shoulder, but it was the fall that killed him.

Tumbleweed turned him over with his boot. So Lee Cherrill was now on his own apart from a gunshot outlaw and two Mexicans.

Cherrill was dangerous with the instinct of an animal. Already he would be waiting. The shots had robbed them of surprise.

The Indian loomed close. At the first shot he'd disappeared into the shadows working around the gunman but was too late to locate him before the final shootout. He was furious with himself.

'I should have figured they would pull that trick. Wait until we were sure of ourselves and then open up. He sure wasn't there when I took a look around.'

He stooped over the body. 'I wonder if there's a poster out for this one? We'll stash him and take him back.' He glanced at the other bodies, emotionless. 'A pity about old Mort. He deserved better and as for the boy...' He spat and turned away and leapt in one movement on to his horse.

Maria, standing back but listening, looked at the bodies and then at Tumbleweed who was also preparing to ride.

'You're not riding on before we bury them?'

Tottie looked at her with contempt.

'Look, ma'am, just how much burying would we be doing with Cherrill breathing down our backs? There's only one way in to this valley and this is it. I can vouch for it. Cherrill will be wanting to get on his way with all that cash for himself. He won't wait. He'll shoot his way out if he has to.'

'Then you reckon he'll think we'll sit it out and wait for him,' Tumbleweed cut in before Maria could explode.

'Yeh, that's what he would do. Save cutting across the valley. He'll reckon he knows the valley better than we do. If we go in, he can get around us and get out while we're cutting trail.'

'So what do we do?' Tumbleweed's respect for the breed was high. He had an 'instinct' for putting himself into another man's head.

'We do what he least expects. We start now and move in.'

'What about Maria?'

'We go in on foot. She can look after the horses...'

'You're not leaving me behind! I'm going in with you. I told you why I was coming along and I'm still of the same mind! I want

Cherrill and I'll get first crack at him!'

Tottie sighed and closed his eyes and then looked heavenward.

'She'll slow us up, boss.' He half turned away and then pivoted on his heels. His fist caught her on the point of her chin. It was a calculated blow to knock her out but not kill her. She would have a cracking headache when she woke up. Tumbleweed stared in horror.

'Hell, Tottie, was that necessary?'

Tottie rubbed his knuckles.

'She's a stubborn woman. I don't like her kind. They use their bodies to influence men. They never play fair, and the only way to deal with them is with violence. They understand and respect that.'

'Whatever happens, she's going to be no good to us. I'd best wrap her in a blanket and hide her away. We'll leave the bodies of Mort and the boy nearby and when we return we'll bury 'em. We can't take them and Cherrill back and cope with Maria too.'

Tottie gave a faint smile.

'Always providing we out-think Cherrill!'

Tumbleweed hunched his shoulders.

'Yeh, well, if one of us doesn't make it, the other might; and that bastard is worth five hundred bucks or so Hawkins says. Help me with the bodies and then we'll make Maria comfortable.'

Swiftly they moved and chose a deep crevice of rock just inside the entrance to the valley. They made Maria comfortable and she looked to be out for several hours. In front of her and across the opening of the crevice they laid the bodies of the two men. Hal Clausen they left lying where he fell.

Then, finding a suitable place to tether the horses, they moved off into the valley with silent tread. Tottie did not speak but it was understood between them that now he was in charge for this was his own wild world. They moved at a crouch, stopping and starting at each sound until Tottie straightened and silently pointed and Tumbleweed saw the cabin a few yards in front of them.

'You think he's still inside?' breathed Tumbleweed in Tottie's ear. Tottie shook his head, and pointed to a shadowy rock behind the cabin.

'I think he's behind there, forted up. I saw a movement. I'm going to climb up behind him. You watch out for the others but I don't think he'll reckon much to the Mexes. If the shooting starts, move in quick. Right?'

'Right.' Tumbleweed watched him crawl away for a few yards and then disappear into the shadows.

Tumbleweed moved his position so that he could see the cabin head on. Something didn't smell right to him. It was too quiet, too dead...

Then he heard the gunshot followed by several others and knew that Tottie had been rumbled. He also saw the flicker of flame which suddenly engulfed the log cabin. The glare came from inside. Suddenly the door was flung open and a staggering figure already ablaze came out screaming.

The whine of a bullet and the burning figure dropped. What the hell was happening? Tumbleweed set off at a run. It was an involuntary reaction to reach the burning man but the angry whine of another slug had him leaping and rolling on the ground, his own Colt barking. He let off a couple of snap shots all the while aware of shooting somewhere at the rear of the burning building.

Then he was up and running and dodging and weaving in the glare of the fire which now was well alight. Then a figure humping a saddle-bag was silhouetted in the doorway. It was Cherrill and he was coolly taking aim with his Colt at Tumbleweed as the fire roared behind him.

'Come and get me you bastard, if you

can!' And that was all he heard as something heavy and solid connected to the back of his head.

Tumbleweed awoke with a roaring in his ears and the smell of smoke in his nostrils. He crawled towards the dead man, fingering the lump on the back of his head. For a moment or two he lay gasping. His mouth was dry. He would have given anything for a drink. Then, raising himself up, he saw that the dead man was not a Mex, so he must be Cherrill's outlaw pal who had been gunshot.

All was now quiet, so where the hell was Tottie? And what about the two Mexicans?

The answer came when he crawled round the back of the still smouldering building. The old man and the Mexican woman had been knifed before the fire started. So, what about the boy? And then it came to him. The youth had been detailed by Cherrill to cause a diversion. God knows what story Cherrill had made up to get him up there on that crag and risk his life; probably the promise of all the cash he and his family would ever need in his life.

Then Tumbleweed sat on his heels and thought of himself. The crack on the head ... the youth must have been smarter than Tottie figured and Tottie could be lying

83

dead somewhere.

He struggled upright and after the ground had stopped whirling he weaved his way towards the rocky face that he estimated had been where Tottie had seen movement.

All was still. Dawn was still some time away so that he figured he hadn't been out more than two hours. He stopped to vomit. He had all the signs of concussion. Cursing, he staggered on. The Mex youth had moved like an Indian to come up behind him and bop him one ... an Indian! And then Tumbleweed's heart began to pound. Jesus Christ! It couldn't be! But it was.

He found the Mex youth and he'd been shot in the back. So the other shots had been for his benefit to make it sound like a regular gun battle.

It had been Tottie who'd crept up behind him and knocked him out. He stared grimly ahead. What had happened afterwards? Had he killed Cherrill and made off with the cash himself?

Then another thought rampaged through his mind, and brought him up sharp. What had happened to Maria?

FOUR

Lee Cherrill's great bellow of laughter brought a reluctant smile to Indian Tottie's dark face.

'So we figured right. Hawkins set old Mort and that boy of his up. Who's this guy? We didn't reckon on a stranger.'

'A cocky knowall who rode into town not long before you were due,' answered Tottie, and turned Tumbleweed over with his boot so that Cherrill could see his face. 'Seen him before?'

Cherrill bent over Tumbleweed and took a good look.

'Nope, never seen him before.'

'Name of Tumbleweed. The fool fairly begged for the job of posseing and Shaw-cross was sure glad to take him on. Real dead set on taking you back like a side of beef over your horse,' he finished laconically.

'Was he now? Maybe I should kick his head in for his pains!' He raised his foot to kick him but Tottie gave him a shove.

'Not now, Cherrill. Leave him and let's get

to hell out of here. We've got some burying to do and there's Clausen and old Mort and the boy. We want to leave no evidence of what's gone on here. Shawcross and his pals are mighty powerful and if they get wind of how it happened, then we could be in big trouble.'

'You don't expect us to get away with thirty thousand bucks without those guys adding up the obvious, do you?'

'Ted Ramsey will want us to play it smart. Don't you see the obvious? We can lay it on this feller, Tumbleweed.'

'And how do we do that?'

'Well, as I see it, Lee Cherrill has to be working for someone and that person is a member of the old Quantrill gang, who just happens to be Tumbleweed. Come into town at the right time and practically forced Shawcross to hire him. It figures.'

Lee Cherrill laughed.

'Nothing like the truth that's just a little twisted! It might work. I've already made me a reputation as Lee Cherrill. You and me, Tottie are going to finish up back east smoking fat cigars and rolling the best fancy women and owning a chain of gambling joints and cathouses that would make a bald man's hair curl!'

'There's only one thing, Ted ... Maria's

back there, and she's gunning for Lee Cherrill.'

'Is she, by God? Now that's tough. Makes things a little complicated. Where is she?'

'Back at the entrance. She wanted to move in with us and come after you; and the bitch would have had your guts the moment she set eyes on you. You under estimated her, Ted. I knocked her out and we left her to sleep it off.'

'You mean she's out there alone?'

'Why yes, if you can call it alone being with two stiffs!'

'Well then, there's no problem. I'll get my horse and the mule and we'll go and bury some bodies ... Maria's along with the rest!'

Tottie was silent. He had much to think about, his own woman in particular. Did he want her in his new life? He tried to think of her dressed up like a lady and couldn't imagine it. No, Bet could never be up-rooted. She was going to be part of his past. A pity really. He was fond of Bet and she didn't mind what he did in bed. He'd send her a few bucks. That would put things right. It would mean a new start and the past would be dead.

He was waiting eagerly for Ted Ramsey's return. The saddle-bags were now strapped on the mule. He'd never seen $30,000 all in one go before and the idea awed him. Jesus, what a man could do with the whole of it!

But he put that thought from him. Better half of it and have Ted Ramsey's backing than have all Quantrill's old gang looking to slit his throat. Who knows, there might be other schemes afoot in the future. Ted Ramsey would always find other Shawcrosses to double-cross and he could be part of it.

Ted Ramsey looked at him and grunted, wondering just how much he could trust this half-breed bastard. Breeds had a reputation of belonging to no man; they hunted for themselves. Still, he'd proved his loyalty up until now. There had been two other occasions when Indian Tottie had been useful. Settling with Maria would be the final test. He would let Tottie do what was necessary. He smiled at the thought. Tottie would then be in his power, for everyone knew that Indians were super-stitious and that taking life on someone else's command automatically put the killer at the mercy of the one who instigated the deed. It was like self-hypnosis and despite a white father, Tottie had listened and learned his lessons well at his mother's knee.

He watched Tottie's eyes in the light from

the fast burning cabin but Tottie was too well versed in hiding his thoughts. Ted Ramsey had no idea what was going through his mind.

'Where's your horse? I'm ready to ride.'

Tottie's answer was brief.

'Back at the entrance with the others. What about the Mexes?'

'Shoved them behind the cabin. Any objections?'

Tottie's lips moved in a semblance of a smile.

'Suits me. Saves sweat, digging.'

'If ever this valley was discovered, the grass will have grown over even what's left of the cabin. Couldn't be better.' He paused and as Tottie prepared to run alongside the horse he said softly, 'There's Maria ... will you do the business? It wouldn't be right for me to be the one seeing as we were lovers...'

Tottie's eyes narrowed.

'Since when did you get an attack of goddamn righteousness? It didn't bother you on that last raid and you raped that kid's mother before shooting her!'

Ted Ramsey frowned.

'Are you telling me you're refusing to kill her?'

Tottie shrugged. 'I think a man should do

his own killing. I don't care for the bitch. She's not my kind of woman and if I had a reason for killing her, I'd do it, but she's your problem, mister. You do it!'

'She's your problem too. If something goes wrong, you don't get your cut. She knows me as Lee Cherrill. I don't want all those fancy friends of Shawcross to find out who their associate Ted Ramsey is, or whose coffers their cash has gone into. I've got quite a few ideas before the cow runs dry!'

Tottie stared at him, suddenly contemptuous.

'You're frightened of doing the job! You don't want to look in her eyes as you do it!'

'If that's what you like to think.' Ted Ramsey's lips curled.

'And when it's done I'll be the only one who knows Lee Cherrill is Ted Ramsey and you will have put the big X on me!'

Ramsey laughed.

Tottie couldn't see the expression in Ramsey's eyes. His bellowing laughter masked the sudden tension in him. So Tottie was being smart. He was using his head. He'd been right not to trust him all the way.

'We're buddies, aren't we, Tottie? What's all this about big Xs? And what's this rot about being the only guy who can pinpoint

Ted Ramsey as Cherrill, the outlaw? Come on now, you're part of my plans for the future. You're the one who watches out for my back. I need you, Tottie. Whatever we do in the future, you're the eyes in the back of my head, so let's have no talk of Xs or' – and now his voice sank low and Tottie's imagination filled it with a hidden menace, – 'you being the only one who could betray me. Being buddies, you would never do that, would you, Tottie?'

'Of course not. I was only pointing out...'

'Then don't,' Ramsey cut in roughly. 'I'm the one who thinks and points things out. Now to prove that we've got trust between us, I want you to do that job. Right?'

'Right.' And Ted Ramsey, alias Lee Cherrill, smiled. He could feel the first hint of total power over the breed; a useful power to be manipulated until the first time came when Tottie wasn't needed any more. The smile deepened. Tottie had sure made a mistake if he thought that he wasn't capable of killing Maria Sanchez. He could kill his own mother if he had to...

Two hours later they paused at the entrance of the valley.

'Well? Where the hell did you leave her?'

Tottie looked around. He'd located the

crevice where he and Tumbleweed had carried the bodies. They were still there but there was no sign of Maria nor the blanket in which she had been wrapped.

'She's a tough bitch. She must have come round and panicked because she was lined up with the stiffs. She can't have gone far. I'll take a looksee. Her trail will be fresh and she must have made for the horses.'

'Yeh, you do that. The extra horses will be useful too. We can ride turn and turn about and keep the horses fresh.' Ramsey slid from his own mount and tethered it beside the pack animal.

Tottie eyed the proceedings before moving out. It had crossed his mind that Ramsey might take off during his search for the woman. The first sign of treachery and Tottie would kill him.

As he expected, Maria's mare was missing. The other horses were still tethered on the lariat rope. Now it was a case of following the horse's trail. Again she had done what he expected. The horse's clear footprints trailed him back into the valley. The fool woman was attempting to catch up with himself and Tumbleweed and by the rate of travel she was full of hell and spitting horseshoe nails and she'd veered off the track too for some reason. There was no figuring logic in a woman. That must be why they hadn't come bang on her. They'd passed her some time back.

Cursing, he turned back. They would have to retrace their journey if Ramsey still wanted the girl killed. It was going to put another half day on to their getaway...

Maria Sanchez, thanking her keen hearing and the fact that she had left the soft track for hard stony ground amongst a jumble of boulders, shivered as she nipped her horse's nose and watched the half-breed hesitate and turn back.

It had been a shock to her to see Lee Cherrill and Indian Tottie pass close by in the first place. Her first reaction was to break cover and confront Lee Cherrill and risk a shot, but there would be the half-breed to contend with and she wasn't proficient enough with a gun to get them both. Now she figured on finding out what happened to Tumbleweed.

She moved out when she reckoned Tottie was out of hearing range. She would have to move fast before they came back for she was under no illusions. Lee Cherrill wanted her killed. Any love between them had been on her side. He'd used her and now she was expendable. There would always be other women to be used and cast aside for Lee Cherrill unless ... she gritted her teeth ... unless she made sure that he died...

Tumbleweed was intent on following the clear trail left by Tottie on foot and of Lee Cherrill on horseback and the interesting set of heavily laden mule prints, proof of Cherrill's and Tottie's complicity regarding the bank robbery. The breed surely had him fooled. His head ached and he wished he'd ridden into the valley for his high-heeled riding boots were not designed for walking. He cursed softly to himself as he staggered along.

Maria watched his approach. She and her mare standing a little above the trail on a flat overhanging rock, could see him struggling. She smiled. She could have picked him off so easily if that had been her intention. She called him softly so that her voice should not carry on the still air.

'Tumbleweed, it's Maria.'

Tumbleweed straightened with a jerk and, swaying a little, looked about him until he saw her nearly above him.

'What the hell are you doing here?'

'Looking for you. Do you know that cursed breed is in with Lee Cherrill?'

94

Tumbleweed fingered the lump on the back of his head ruefully.

'I figured it that way when I came round. The bastard cold-cocked me from behind. I still feel cross-eyed.'

Maria allowed her mare to choose its own way down on to the trail. It came down with a sliding motion that loosened dirt and stones and caused a little avalanche. Tumbleweed watched her gloomily.

'I hope the breed's far enough away not to hear your clumsy method of riding! You want lessons in lifting your horse over obstacles and negotiating steep descents like a ballet dancer!'

'You want to be thankful I came looking for you without criticizing my riding. Here, I'll give you a hand. Climb aboard and we'll get after them.' She bent down to him and took his hand. The mare skirmished a little, objecting to the double load but finally settled and trotted back along the trail.

Tumbleweed allowed his head to drop. He was in a much worse state than he would admit even to himself. The scent of her kept his senses fully aware however. No man however whoozy, could allow himself to slip into oblivion beside such a soft luscious body.

The whine of a rifle slug whistling past

them brought him violently into the present, and he reacted without thought. Grabbing Maria's light body he flung her to the ground and rolled after her. The mare whinnied and kicked out and galloped away.

Maria, winded, could only lie where she had fallen while Tumbleweed rolled behind a small boulder and blazed away in the direction of the first shot.

'Get under cover fast,' he rapped, 'and then toss me your gun. I'll cover while you load up again.'

He snapped off another two shots and then tossed her his empty weapon while without a word, Maria made herself as small as possible and threw him her gun.

Again came two rifleshots close fired. One splatted the boulder beside him and the other ploughed into the hard ground.

'How you making out?' he shouted to Maria.

'All done but I'm low on shells.'

'Goddamit! We walked into this lot. My brains weren't working. Look, I'm going to toss you my gunbelt and one of my guns. You keep blazing away and I'm going to try and get behind the bastards. We'll never get out of here otherwise.'

Maria swallowed. This wasn't the time to

go all-over weak. She allowed herself a grin.

'If I don't make it, promise me you'll kill him?'

'Honey, if it's the last thing I do, I'll stiff him and it won't only be for you...'

'What...?' But he was gone and she forgot his words as she answered the intermittent firing. Panic turned to real fear when she felt the sting as of a wasp and looked and saw the top of her shoulder grazed and bleeding. Whoever was up there on the opposite crag was beginning to get his bearings...

Tumbleweed bellied away using knees and elbows to snake his way through the undergrowth. He moved upwards and around until he figured he could watch and locate the half-breed for he was in no doubt it was he. There was only one man out there unless he was very much mistaken. Tottie would be doing the dirty work while Lee Cherrill watched his saddle-bags. The sound of the repeating rifle came spasmodically giving him some idea of where the breed would be. Maria was keeping up an answering barrage. He felt a growing admiration for her pluck in the face of danger. The rifle spat again and this time there was no answering fire.

He moved faster. Maybe Maria had stopped a slug ... something more to feed the hate he was feeling for the traitorous breed. Then the sharp splat of the Colt came again and he realized that Maria had been loading up. Good old Maria!

Then the rifle barked just ahead and Tumbleweed came to his feet and crouching low, gun ready, took the last few yards at a run.

He saw Tottie just below him, hunkered behind a jagged boulder. He raised his gun to fire; he had no compunction in shooting him in the back; this was no time for ethics. He watched Tottie take deliberate aim with the rifle and rage filled him. He snapped off a shot but Tottie's recoil from the gun blast saved his life. Tumbleweed's slug shattered the rifle barrel and it exploded into fragments and Tottie screamed with pain as a piece of metal dug deep into his hand.

He turned like a cornered rat and with teeth bared met Tumbleweed's lunge with fists swinging and a booted foot aiming for Tumbleweed's crotch.

Tumbleweed saw it coming and caught his ankle, twisting it sharply and again Tottie screamed. Then, lashing out with both feet, the breed caught Tumbleweed in the stomach, making him gasp and cough.

Tottie aimed a kick at his head as he lay

helpless and just as he made contact, Tumbleweed heaved himself up, taking an ugly graze that drew blood and then he was on Tottie again hands about his throat.

'You bastard!' Tumbleweed croaked, and squeezed as hard as his diminishing strength would allow. 'I'll cut your bloody liver out!' And then they were rolling over and over, gasping snorting and great gobs of sweat blinding both of them.

Then Tottie was astride and groping found a loose stone with one hand while holding Tumbleweed down with his knee. Tumbleweed squirmed and heaved to toss him from him. He saw the stone and it looked as big as his head. It was crashing down when he heaved in desperation. Tottie lost his balance and Tumbleweed scrabbled amongst the dried dirt and flung a handful into Tottie's eyes.

Tottie rolled away holding his face and cursing. Then, managing to look at the now still Tumbleweed, he saw what was in Tumbleweed's eyes.

'You're not going to shoot me down in cold blood?'

'Why not?'

Tottie shrugged. 'You didn't put me in mind of a cold-blooded killer!'

'No? You're a very poor judge of character, mister!'

Tumbleweed raised his Colt slowly and the breed saw the killer look in his eyes. He grabbed for his handgun still in its holster but he was dead before he could draw it.

Maria watched him as moved towards her. He was bleeding from several cuts and the report from the last shot had been ominous. She shivered, her courage now gone and reaction was setting in.

'He's dead, isn't he?'

Tumbleweed's glance was harsh. He did not answer nor did he need to. It was there in every movement.

'What about Lee?'

He threw her a level glance.

'You feel the same way as you said?'

She nodded. 'I was never more sure in my life. What about him up there?' She indicated in the direction he'd come from.

'Covered his body under a pile of stones. It was the least I could do.'

Maria sighed.

'There was no sign of Lee?'

'None. All was quiet as the grave, no pun intended. I think he took off while the breed was gunning for us. We've got no choice. We'll have to stick with him, Maria, unless you want me to go on alone? I'll get him, never fear!'

His look was level as he faced her. He waited for her decision. It meant ... well, it meant something different than it might mean for her.

'You think I can't keep up?'

'I didn't say that but it could be tough. We'd be alone...' he paused, and then said softly, 'I'm human, Maria. It would be hard riding during the day, and at night...'

'You might want to cuddle up to me?'

'Something like that.'

'You wouldn't always treat me like a man?'

He gave a sudden quick smile.

'You can't forgive me for that, can you? I admit I was wrong and was a fool to think such a thing never mind say it. Now, I reckon I'll treat you as you want me to treat you.'

'You really mean that? You'd leave me alone if I wanted it that way?'

He nodded but choked a little under his breath. He was gambling that she was as passionate with her sexual favours as she was with her temper.

'My mind's still made up. I'm coming with you.' She gave him a provocative smile. 'Who knows? Circumstances might make it possible...' She lifted a shoulder to him and laughing, turned away to hide the look in her eyes.

He grinned. Maybe chasing Lee Cherrill was going to turn out the best decision of his life.

Maria interrupted his thoughts by returning to clean his wounds which fortunately were only superficial. There was a certain amount of bruising which rather spoilt his features but Maria was gentle and Tumbleweed enjoyed the touch of her hands. It hadn't been often in his life since he'd lost his wife and family that anyone had cared enough to succour him.

When she finished he caught her wrist and drew her to him, her scent heady in his nostrils.

'Thank you, Maria; you are a very caring woman under that violent exterior. A woman a man would be proud to have at his side.' He kissed her gently and then his other arm went about her waist and his kiss deepened until she pushed him away.

'You can stop right there, mister. I would clean up my mare in the same way I cleaned you if it was necessary.' Now her tone hardened. 'I'm going along with you because you are my only hope of finding Lee Cherrill. Right?'

'Right! You're a cock-teasing little bitch, but I stick by what I said. Now what are you waiting for? Let's find those mounts and get riding!'

Much later they found the bodies of old Mort and young Drydon. They had been moved and searched and the horses nearby had been freed for their lariat rope was slashed. But they were in luck for the horses had grouped together and were feeding on the only lush pasturage close by.

A hastily dug grave and a few words quickly spoken and they were on their way, Maria subdued at the wanton loss of life and Tumbleweed angry that Cherrill had found time to stop and rob the dead of cash and old Mort's watch.

Cherrill had not tried to hide his tracks. He had been very sure of not being followed. Maybe he hoped that the breed and Tumbleweed would kill each other after Tottie killed Maria. At best if Tottie survived, it would have been a waste of time trying to hide from Tottie who was the best tracker in those parts.

The sun was high in the sky and Maria exhausted when Tumbleweed called a halt. They had no meat but plenty of coffee and salt and flour. Tumbleweed's glance took in the apparent state of Maria.

'Lie in the shade and I'll rustle up what grub there is. We're on short rations but I'll go hunt us something later.' He spoke briefly and to the point and did not wait for an answer. There was plenty of grass so he suspected a spring close by. He wandered off to take a looksee and to give Maria time to do what she had to do behind a boulder.

He had not only found a spring but also a pool which looked to be a gathering place for wild animals. It would make a good place to hide for catching them some meat. He would come back at sundown.

The coffee-pot full of water and his hat filled for one of the horses he made his way back and found that Maria had not rested as he'd ordered but found enough dry scrub to start a fire. It smouldered and she fanned the flame. Even in her exhaustion she appeared graceful and the hint of bosom as she bent over the fire made him catch his breath. He'd been too long without a woman he reflected morosely, and he could do without this inner tumult, like a man with a tomahawk sticking out of his head.

Without a word he measured out coffee and settled it on the sticks and then went to get their precious flour and salt. Soon there was a wafting of coffee on the slight breeze that teased his stomach and gave him something else to think about.

He mixed dough, slopping some of their precious water he'd saved from the coffee-pot and slapped it into small round thin tortillas before putting each piece into a battered black frying pan that stank of rank grease.

'Anything wrong?'

Maria, seeing that Tumbleweed was as good as his word and was prepared to get the food had sat down with a relief she could barely hide. It was proving a little too much for her to keep up with the man's gruelling pace and for the hours he drove them both. But she wouldn't give in. She wasn't going to use the excuse of being a woman. After all, she'd insisted on coming on this manhunt.

The hate for Lee Cherrill sustained her. She lived with it, tasted it and it had become part of her. No man would ever use her again as a sex object, tire of her and finally decide to have her killed like an animal he regarded just as rightful prey...

Now she watched Tumbleweed do what had to be done. Again she asked, 'Anything wrong?'

For a moment she thought he wasn't

going to answer. She had never regarded him as a moody man, so something must be bugging him.

Then he looked directly at her.

'It was a mistake you coming along in the first place. I should have put my foot down, ridden out before you were aware of it. If you followed it would have been at your own risk.' He spoke savagely and hurled the words at her.

'What have I done? Hell, I've kept up with you. I haven't held you back, I haven't complained. I'm just another man...'

'But you're not, are you? Even bundled up in those men's clothes, you're still all woman!'

'Ah ... now I see...' 'A glimmer of a smile came over her face. 'I thought we'd made a pact. You want to go back on it?'

'No! Of course not! Well ... maybe ... I don't know. You're having a hell of an effect on my tackle. Hell! I shouldn't be talking like that. You're not one of the usual fancy women. I know you were Cherrill's woman but you never hawked it about for money. I'm sorry, but you've got a feller's insides boiling away so the steam's going to bust loose at any time! You're not safe around me, Maria. I might do something I've never done before in my life.'

Maria regarded him gravely.

'I'm not quite understanding you, Tumbleweed. Are you talking about being with a woman or are you talking about rape?'

He flushed.

'Hell! I've been with plenty of women, but they've been willing, and I was once married...' He stopped abruptly. 'But that's another story and one I never repeat,' he went on, 'so don't ask me about it. I'm talking about rape, if you must know. I know how you feel...'

'Do you?' Suddenly the words hung on in the air between them like flags.

His glance was as grave as her own.

'Well, I think I do.' And he dived for the coffee-pot that had slipped and the coffee was sizzling into the fire.

'You'd better watch that panbread too,' she broke in, 'it smells a little burned. I think I should have done it.'

Pensively she watched as he rescued the pan bread and poured two tin mugs of coffee. She reached for hers and felt his hand tremble as her fingers brushed his. She sipped, burning her tongue then said softly, 'How long is it, Tumbleweed?'

He looked puzzled.

'How long ... you know, how long since

you were with a woman?'

He swallowed. 'Long enough.'

She laughed and the sound echoed around them. 'Then it's time you got some kind of relief!'

'What about you?'

'Me? I suppose I'm missing Lee. I think you and I should help each other...'

Tumbleweed swallowed a gulp of scalding coffee and never felt it as he watched her unbutton her shirt and bare her pointed breasts.

Then, breathing hard, he threw away the mug and he was helping her to pull off the ugly canvas trousers revealing the smooth golden body of her. Heart thumping as if he would choke, he buried his head into the warmth of her and for a time both of them forgot the reason why they were together...

FIVE

He awoke and automatically reached for her but she was gone. Already he wanted her again. Her scent and warmth was all about him. He stretched luxuriously. He hadn't felt so relaxed or on the top of the world for a long time. She was a great lover and had given him whatever he'd wanted. She'd pleased herself too and he knew he'd fulfilled all her own desires. She was some woman and he would go all out to keep her. She would change his life. He would no longer be a drifter. Tumbleweed need not exist any more. He could revert to Jim Weldon and start a new life. But there was still Ted Ramsey. Before settling down with Maria, always providing she liked the idea, he would have to seek out Ramsey and he was well on the way to doing so. If he took Cherrill back to San Paulo then he was bound to meet Ramsey as one of the bank's sponsors and an associate of Shawcross's. He decided to wait before putting any ideas in Maria's way. She might even think he was pushing her.

He got up out of their blankets to go look for her. The shadows were already lengthening. Lovemaking and sleeping had taken up much time, but he felt more rested for the interlude. He grinned as he watched her bathing in the small muddy pool. It was already churned up with her movements as she washed her long hair and dived beneath the surface. Once again he lusted after the smooth breasts and shoulders that rose every now and again to tease him.

Then she caught his eye and laughed and waved to him.

'Come in, sleepy head and wash all that stink off you. It's lovely and cold and it'll make a man of you!'

'I'm a man already, look!' And she did and she laughed again.

'Come in and let's do it in the water. Have you ever done it that way?'

He shook his head. 'I have a feeling I'll wither away!'

'Not when I'm here to do the necessary! Come on, I dare you!' With that he jumped in beside her and he gasped at the cold.

'Jesus! It must be mountain water! You little bitch! You fooled me.'

'Have I?' Then she was all over him like a leech, ducking him and rubbing his back with some soapwort she'd found growing at the side of the pool. It foamed a little and her hands felt good on his back and then on his chest and finally at his thighs and it was then he found that she had not fooled him and he was as good as he'd ever been ... and even better as her legs twined around him and they laughed and whirled about in the water like two otters.

He carried her back to their camp and

kissed her as he set her down.

They stood like Adam and Eve, arms entwined unaware of what was going on around them. Then one of the horses whinnied and Tumbleweed's head came up with a jerk but he was too late, a slug slammed into the boulder behind them. Tumbleweed cursed and threw Maria to the ground.

'What ... where?' gasped Maria as she hugged the ground.

Tumbleweed did not answer, he was too busy lunging for his rifle which fortunately was only a couple of feet away.

'For God's sake, keep your head down,' he snapped and raked the thick scrub surrounding the waterhole.

Another shot had Tumbleweed dropping to the ground and this time a small paunchy figure with a sweaty straggled beard stepped out grinning and waving a business-like Winchester.

'Make a move, buster, and I'll ruin that rutting pole before I kill you!'

'What do you want?'

'What do you expect?' And he indicated Maria. 'She gives a rare nice performance and it's given me some ideas. I want her. I want the woman!' His voice went coldly grim.

111

'What do you say if I don't let you?'

'I don't say anything; I just do. You, get yourself over here and let's have a feel of you. It's been months...'

He jerked his head at Maria who cowered further down in the dirt.

'What are you going to do when you're at it? How are you going to stop me from getting you?'

The man rasped his beard. 'I've got my gun. I'll kill her if you make a move!'

'No you wouldn't. You wouldn't want to lose her body. What if I let you have her and then you let us go? Can't say fairer than that.'

'Tumbleweed!' But Tumbleweed ignored Maria's scream.

'Well, what about it, mister? Better a good ride without worrying about your back. I'll honour the bargain if you will!'

The man looked suspiciously at Tumble-weed.

'You're kidding, aren't you?'

'Why should I? I've only known the bitch for a few days. She's nothing to me. I've met as good or better in Abilene or Tucson. Mind you,' – as he saw Maria's scowl – 'she's better than any Mex women I've been with. By the way, I don't know your name.'

'Does it matter? I ran with Quantrill's new gang and I'm looking for a guy who's been seen in these parts who was one of Quantrill's own trusted men before he died. You're not one of Quantrill's men, are you?'

'What if I said I was?'

'Well, in that case we could share the woman. We could shake hands on the deal.'

'Who's the guy you're looking for?'

'Oh, to hell ... why waste time on all that crap? I want the woman now, and by the look of you both, I can't wait much longer!'

'Right! Maria, get moving. Go and do what you can for the poor bastard who is thirsty as I was!'

Dumbly Maria looked at Tumbleweed. His left eye flickered and suddenly a surge of relief swept through her.

'Tumbleweed, must I...?'

'Stand up, Maria, and let him have a good look at you so that he can enjoy what he's going to get,' he interrupted roughly, and Maria gasped, her relief subsiding at his tone.

She slowly stood up and faced the stranger. His eyes ravished her and he licked his lips in anticipation.

'Go on now, point those breasts and suck in that waist and make it a good show.' Tumbleweed's mocking tone made her angry

113

and she proudly stared at the man with shoulders straight and heart palpitating.

The stranger took a step forward, oblivious to Tumbleweed, his grasping hands moving spasmodically to touch the smooth flesh and it was the last thought he ever had.

Tumbleweed shot him through the forehead.

He caught Maria as she collapsed sobbing and held her to him stroking her hair, very aware of her trembling body. He felt a great anger flooding through him for allowing himself to be so carried away by his own lust that he'd forgotten the first rule of survival.

'Maria, forgive me. I should never have let all this happen. He could have killed us both and we wouldn't have known anything about it! If he'd been an Indian...' His voice trailed away as he thought of his crass stupidity. He shuddered.

She looked up at him, eyes still glazed with shock at the suddenness of it all, and then glanced at the body.

'We'll have to bury him. He was so repulsive.' And she too shuddered at what might have been. Then, embarrassed at their nakedness, she said softly, 'Thank you for saving me from...' She buried her face into his chest and his arms tightened about her, still angry at his foolishness.

'Get yourself dressed and we'll move out,' he said gruffly, 'after I've planted him. I don't think even his own mother would miss him!'

He released her without looking at her again and took his clothes and after hastily dressing went to examine the body. Already the flies were crawling over the face and exploring the nostrils while the eyes stared unblinkingly up at him.

It took an hour's sweat to scoop out the hard ground to a depth that would take the body. He was glad when the last stone was piled on top of the mound. He knew that the grave wouldn't remain intact for long. His rotting body would attract predators, and soon it would be exposed and dragged away and fought over by ravening coyotes. But at least Maria's womanly feelings would be satisfied.

They moved out, not waiting for Tumble-weed to hunt for meat. Both only had one thing in mind, to get away from the scene of humiliation. The memory of it scalded both their minds and it would take some time to forget.

As they rode on, Maria kept looking up

and around, puzzled and increasingly excited. At last she turned to Tumbleweed.

'I'm sure we're not so far from the border. If the light wasn't fading so fast I'd say that the shape of those hills in the distance reminds me of the hills at the back of Grandfather's ranch. I wonder if Cherrill is making his way there!'

Tumbleweed pulled up his horse and rested on the pommel and looked about him. The sun was going down fast and shadows were lengthening, then he mopped his brow and eased his sweaty hat.

'I don't think you can really tell, Maria. Lots of hills look the same and we're a hell of a way from the border.'

'Not so far as you think! Don't forget, I was born just over the border and it's my home ground. It smells like home! It's in the air around us!'

Tumbleweed smiled at her passion. 'Now why would Cherrill make for your ranch?'

'Because it's safe and it's high in the hills and it's easy to guard. Also my grandfather knows him.'

'And so?'

'He's frightened of him, Tumbleweed. He'll do anything Cherrill tells him to do! He'll wait until all the fuss dies down and then his idea will be to start again somewhere he's not known. He used to laugh and say that he had a sure bolt-hole if things got tough.'

'You mean he's already made a niche for himself somewhere?'

'Yes, I'm sure of it.'

'Huh, then we must press on or maybe we'll miss him altogether. I hope you're right, Maria about where he's heading. I'm leaving it in your hands.'

She gave him a little triumphant grin.

'So I'm being useful after all!'

He had the grace to flush, and then he too, grinned.

'One up to you, Maria. Maybe, you're going to be my only hope of catching the bastard.'

Maria took a deep breath, then, 'Look, I'm willing to take a gamble if you are. I'm so sure I'm right, that we can leave his trail and I can find a short cut through those hills. It's an old Indian trail not known except by those born and bred in the hills.'

Tumbleweed shrugged.

'I've already told you I'm in your hands. If you're that sure, what are we waiting for?'

'It means a short sharp climb up and over that peak after we cross the river. But we'll be over the border and we'll be on the way to

Indian Lodge Pass. There are a number of Indians living around the Pass and that's why it's not used very much. My grandmother was one of them and Grandfather has always dealt fairly with them. They will help us if we need assistance.'

'If that's the way it is, then let's get at it.' And so, twisting and turning and picking their way through scrub and twisty canyons they moved nearer to the river and to the ever-looming hills.

At last they drew up on a high promontory and watched the white foaming waters of the Rio Grande which, because of a narrowing of the gorge, flowed faster than normal.

'How the hell do we pass over that lot?' Tumbleweed asked in wonder. He'd never seen such rapids. Maria smiled.

'We follow the river a little way until it widens and becomes calmer, and you will see an old Indian swing bridge. It is only wide enough to take one man and his horse at a time. It looks frail but it will also take a loaded mule, so you need not be frightened.'

Tumbleweed straightened his back.

'If you can risk it, I will.'

Maria smiled. 'I knew you would say that.'

They followed the faintest of trails along the river. By all the signs it was not used

118

much and Tumbleweed saw why when they reached the point where they could see the bridge. It sure looked unsafe in the moonlight. He drew a sharp breath and sweat broke out on his forehead. No one in his right mind would cross that bridge, or only if it was essential.

'Is there no other way?' His voice sounded husky even in his own ears. She glanced at him and laughed.

'Having second thoughts?'

'Well ... if there's another way...'

'There is. Ten miles farther down the river, but this is the way to go to come to the ranch before Cherrill.' Her voice hardened. 'If you won't risk it, I'll go alone. I've crossed it before and I'll do it again. Anything to catch up with that bastard!'

Tumbleweed didn't regard himself as a brave man. He'd never had to prove himself to anyone or even himself. Now, he swallowed a hard lump in his throat. Oh, to hell! He could only die once if his horse panicked and he would rather plunge into the fast-flowing river below than get shot in the back.

'If you go, I go,' he muttered and spurred his horse in front of her to ride the last of the trail towards where twisted vine ropes held the swaying footbridge.

'We'll wait until sunrise,' Maria commanded. 'We'll eat and rest and then when daylight comes we'll take it slow and sure.'

By mutual consent they sat apart, still awkward as to what had happened between them earlier. Now, coolly looking back, Tumbleweed couldn't believe how easy it had been and dared not think of the satisfaction they'd given each other, for fear that his resolve not to touch her again would be broken.

He wondered how she felt but she looked cool and serene and he knew she had a strong inner strength that he had never thought a woman could have. He was in awe of her, respected her like he'd never respected any woman, not even his wife.

Time dragged but at last the first rays of the new day were lengthening and the clear, high-mountain air made seeing much easier. It was Tumbleweed who stirred first and began to pack the few essentials they had used for a dry camp. Now he wished he'd taken time out to hunt for his body craved meat. Maybe there would be an opportunity after they'd crossed this pesky river...

The bridge wobbled and his horse threw up its head and neighed with fright and it was a struggle calming him down so that he would put one foot in front of the other. He spoke softly in a sing-song tone and caressed the soft velvety muzzle and then slid his bandanna from his neck and held it over the horse's eyes and so blinkered him.

Then with a low word to Maria to stay and not follow until he would come back and help her, he moved across the frighteningly narrow bridge one stride at a time leading the nervous animal.

In the middle of the swaying bridge, he stopped, the horse quivering and tossing its head. Quietly, he waited until the sway ceased before moving on. He was soaked in sweat and it wasn't from the heat from the sun but from his own fear.

Then with a feeling of relief that made his knees weak, he was moving on to firm ground. He tethered the horse and turned to go back and face the ordeal again and found Maria halfway across. His heart jumped into his throat as he watched her gentle her mare and crooning, persuade her to move forward in a smooth even flow. He moved to go and meet her but Maria waved him back and he realized that walking towards her and the mare, might upset the animal and so he watched her slow progress.

Suddenly he was doing something he

hadn't done for years. He was praying.

Then he was reaching out for her and drawing her well away from the edge of the gorge and with firm hands, guiding the plucky little mare on to hard ground.

Tethering her swiftly beside his own horse, he took Maria into his arms and they stood entwined and trembling for several minutes.

Then stroking her head, he said softly, 'I never want to see you in such danger again!'

It was some time before they recovered enough to ride on and Tumbleweed took the opportunity to give the horses the last of the oats and measured amounts of water after examining their legs and feet for signs of injury suffered on the gruelling ride. Both seemed fit and were fast recovering and ready and willing to move on. Maria's mare nickered and rubbed her head under Tumbleweed's questing hand. It was a relief that both horses were hard fit, due to the small amount of oats given to each animal.

Nobody knew better than Tumbleweed that a horse was a man's best friend. A fit horse meant the difference between life and death in the harsh lands of the west.

They made good time in the early morning. When the first heat haze lifted Maria pointed joyously.

'Look! You see I'm right. There's the Seven Sisters range and beyond that, the Needle Point.' He could just discern a huge jagged grey shape that slashed the air as it reared up tall and majestic above the surrounding hills. He counted the peaks of the rolling hills and there were seven. He turned to her admiringly.

'You sure know your own country. Have you travelled much in it? I thought you womenfolk stayed close to home.'

'I used to visit my Indian relatives with Grandfather. He said it was good that they should know me. Some of the land is Grandfather's and so the Indians look out for us. They protect our interests.' Suddenly she was silent and looked far ahead and Tumbleweed wondered of what she was thinking.

Then she faced him squarely.

'I made a big mistake with Lee,' she said quietly. 'None of my Indian relatives liked him. Those at the ranch made it clear and they sent out drum messages. But I thought I knew best. Now I know they were right. Lee Cherrill won't be safe in this country.'

'You think they will get him?'

'No. They will respect him as long as they think he is my man, but if they find out otherwise, then his life is worth nothing. But

123

I want him first!' Her head came up and he could see the untamed Indian in her. He said nothing. He wasn't going to argue with a woman who had such a fixed obsession. It would be futile and time-consuming.

They finally hit a broad well-travelled trail that cut across a flat well-watered valley and Maria grinned and spurred her mare and the mare smelling home ground lengthened her stride and Tumbleweed's horse quickened its pace and followed at a thundering gallop.

Far down the valley they could see the winding track that veered to the left and on up and up, but it was now a distinct trail and Tumbleweed did not need telling that the way led up to the high sierra where her grandfather's ranch lay snug and safe.

They were nearly to the top of the winding road when a flat-bottomed wagon came careering round a jutting out boulder and they pulled up with a jerk as the swaying vehicle threatened to cannon into them. The brakes squealed as the wooden shoes hit the wheels, twisting and turning the wheels as the mules pulling the wagon reared and fought the reins as old Pig Whistle hauled with all his strength to bring them to a full stop.

He still smelled like rotten fish and his old

sweaty bearded face poked out from under the shadow of the awning above him.

'Well, if it ain't that young feller from San Paulo!' He smiled showing yellow and broken teeth. Then he eyed Maria more closely. 'And if it ain't the young woman whose brother I delivered up yonder to that eagles' nest up there,' and he nodded in the direction of the sombre hills behind them.

Maria leaned forward.

'My brother! How is Carlos?'

She relaxed when the old man smiled.

'I kept him alive, miss. I put a poultice of moss on his wound. He had a bad fever all the way to the ranch which was a good thing. He never felt the bumps. Soon as we got him home that fat Mex cook of yours took him in hand. She's a rare one is that! Had him bullied something chronic that she did, but she got him so spitting mad that he up and threatened to belt her and damn me, she only smiled, and from that moment he started getting better. How she did it, I don't know.' He shook his head in disbelief. 'She be a rare one and it's only pity she has a man of her own. I would have fair took her on!'

Maria relaxed and sighed with relief and closed her eyes for a moment.

'Thanks be to the good God!' She crossed

herself. 'I hardly dared think of him. I would never have forgiven myself if he had died because I persuaded him to come with us. I really trusted Lee Cherrill...'

'Lee Cherrill?' shouted the old man. 'A pox on him! He came in last night on a near dead horse and raved and shouted until the old one nearly had a heart attack! Demanded a couple of your grandfather's best horses to ride relay. There was somewhere he wanted to go in a hell of a hurry. He got a shock when he saw me and I got a bigger one! The bastard took a potshot at me and put another hole in my old hat.' He took off his battered hat and poked a finger through a new hole.

'You're lucky to be alive,' Maria said sharply. 'Is that why you were coming at a run? Is he out there after you now?'

'Naw ... your grandfather lashed out and spoilt his aim for a second shot when he saw how things were. I was ready to roll anyway. Horses in their traces and just getting the last water butt filled. So I didn't wait to argue, I just lit out at a run and these here mules kicked up their heels and flew. 'Twas natural like, for they'd been eating and resting for a few days and they're mighty fit. I couldn't hold 'em, and believe me, I didn't want to! I want to put as much distance between me and that mad bastard as I can. I wouldn't go up there if I were you, mister!'

Tumbleweed studied Pig Whistle carefully.

'Would you hole up and hang around if you was offered twenty bucks?'

The old man's eyes gleamed. 'Twenty bucks? Now that's a sight of money for just hanging around. Now why should I do that?'

'Because you could be very useful if the little lady here needed to send a message to her relatives.'

'And who might they be?'

'The local mountain Indians...' Maria cut in. 'Have you heard of Chief Cochicata?' Pig Whistle blanched under the dirt. 'He is my second cousin on my grandmother's side.'

'Hell, miss, you don't expect me to face him cold sober? He'll split my head wide open before I could open my mouth!'

'He wouldn't because I should give you a totem to hold high. It is our own signal for help. We have this arrangement. We help them and they help us. Simple.'

'But he could make a mistake...'

Maria scowled. She was fast losing her temper.

'Look, old man, we are wasting time. Either you stay or you go. There are others who would be willing to help us.'

PigWhistle scratched his sparse grey locks and then planted his hat back firmly on his head.

'Aw, to hell, miss, twenty bucks is twenty bucks! If you say I won't get scalped then I'll just have to believe you. But mind you, I want that dough right now!'

Tumbleweed handed over the cash reluctantly. He didn't know if he could trust the old coot not to cut and run before they reached the rancho.

'What you want that I should do?'

'Stash that wagon and hole up the mules and get yourself up there behind the rocks and watch the trail,' Maria said firmly, as if she was bossing her grandfather's field hands. 'If you see a young boy coming hell for leather, step out and meet him. He'll be carrying a totem and you shift your arse fast and make for that peak up there.' She pointed to a lonely outcrop of rock which was curiously flat on top. 'Face due south and wave that totem until you get an answer.'

'And how will I know when I get an answer?'

'You'll hear two gunshots in quick succession and then a third after the count of thirty seconds. Got that?'

The old man nodded vigorously.

'Aye, I've got all that. Anything else?'

'No. Just keep hidden for the hills will be crawling with Mescaleros keeping a lookout on all the trails and anyone caught up will be held until Cochicata looks them over after having a pow-pow with Grandfather or myself. You savvy that?'

'I sure do. I'm no hero, miss, as you remember. I'll sure keep my head down.'

'Then, Tumbleweed, let's ride and we'll see what Lee Cherrill's up to.'

What Lee Cherrill had been up to was way beyond the worst imaginings of either Maria or the more hardened Tumbleweed.

As they walked their horses into the yard, all was quiet. No one ran out to greet them as expected. Neither was there gunfire or the least sign of danger. Tumbleweed felt a cold chill up his back. The silence was brooding and then they came upon the body of old Eduardo Sanchez, already stiff in the sunlight. He was lying where he had fallen when he'd saved Pig Whistle's life. His skull was smashed and a knife wound in the chest had oozed blood after a knife had been wrenched from it.

In the doorway of the rancho, the fat Mex cook, Carmen, lay rigid in death and a faint drone of insects made it clear that already they were feasting.

Tumbleweed found the old stockman slumped inside the blacksmith's shop and nearby, his son, who looked as if he had tried to protect his father.

Tumbleweed's face became grimmer at each revelation until the muscles of his cheeks and neck ached and pure rage rose in him like bile.

He strode over to the house.

'Maria?'

He heard her sobbing and found her in a small back room. She was kneeling at Carlos' bed; a broad-bladed knife standing upright in Carlos' chest, his hands still clasping it as he had tried to draw it out as he had died.

Maria turned to Tumbleweed, distraught. She reached for him and he took her in his arms.

'Why?' she wept. 'Why kill them all?'

SIX

Maria's eyes were dull, the rims red with crying. She handed Tumbleweed a plate of stew and then offered a hunk of fresh-baked cornbread to go with it. The smell of coffee brewing on the old black stove did nothing to stir his tastebuds. He ate for strength not for enjoyment.

She had busied herself about the familiar kitchen that was somehow so different without old fat Carmen fussing around. It had taken her mind off Tumbleweed who'd had the unpleasant job of digging graves. She had come to him when finally the bodies were interred and bowed her head as Tumbleweed stumbled through a few words that dignified their passing.

Silently they ate, but full of their own thoughts, then suddenly Maria's head came up with a jerk.

'Roberto! I forgot about Roberto! He wasn't with the others.'

Tumbleweed looked up from wiping his plate clean with the last of his bread.

'Who's Roberto?'

'Carmen's grandson. He looked after the milk cows and the young calves. Tumbleweed, he may be lying out somewhere hurt! We'll have to find him.'

'Hey, now, don't go off half-cocked. We've got to get a message to Cochicata and it's going to have to be me or you.'

She put out a hand to him.

'Tumbleweed please ... I've known Roberto ever since he was a baby since Carmen brought him here when his mother died. He's a quiet sensitive boy and he would be terrified if he knew what was going on. We can't leave here before we know what's happened to him.'

Tumbleweed sighed. Women! One minute she wanted to be away breathing down Cherrill's neck, next minute she wanted to stick around and look for some fool kid who might well be dead and already stinking to high heaven. Then it would mean another burial and his back was mighty sore as it was from breaking hard ground.

'You're the boss. I suppose if you want to waste time we can do it together. You go and meet Pig Whistle and make sure he moves his arse right quick and sends off that signal, or would you like to climb that peak yourself?' he finished with a grin.

'I might just do that an' all! You will take a looksee for Roberto? You wouldn't fool me, Tumbleweed?'

'Hell! I've done some very queer things in my time, but I don't go back on my word. I'll do the best I can. Do you have any ideas on where to look?'

'There's a pasture tucked away beyond that fall of rock you can just see from the door, a little to the right. He used to take the milking cows out there. We kept the calves in the little corral at the back here, and when the cows came home, they didn't need any driving. They came looking for their calves.'

'So! Well, when I looked around I saw three cows huddled together and two calves and one dead one which had been messed about. I think Cherrill took a chunk of fresh meat with him.'

They stared at each other and then Maria faltered,

'Then Roberto was here...' She choked and then fled outside and Tumbleweed heard her being sick.

He strode outside and held her by the shoulders.

'Hey, there, this is no time to go all womanly over me! Maria!' he barked, and lightly slapped her face twice. Her head rocked as her cheeks stung. Fury exploded in her and she clawed at him.

'How dare you hit me? I should kill you for that!' Tumbleweed, anticipating the move, gripped her wrists and held her firmly. He grinned.

'Now that's better. You can't feel two emotions at once. You can kick my arse if you like and use me as a punchbag but get out there and get Cochicata here as fast as you can and don't write Roberto off as dead until we find his body. Now git!'

He was more perturbed than he liked to admit. One thing Maria had not thought of was that Cherrill might have taken Roberto with him for a reason. He was carrying bulky money bags and Pig Whistle had told them that he had picked out old Sanchez' two best horses to ride relay. So, wherever he was going, he was going fast. He also might have realized how valuable Roberto was to get across a country infested with the Mescaleros. As Roberto was part of the Sanchez household, the Mescaleros would hesitate to shoot if Roberto was being held in front of Cherrill. But once out of the territory, Cherrill would feel safe and then he could kill Roberto for he could ride faster alone.

The first thing to do was to look again in all the outbuildings, for the earlier search had been for Cherrill and he would have come out shooting. Now Tumbleweed took his time. He searched the blacksmith's shop, the small shacks of Carmen and the Mexican couple, the shed where a number of tools were stacked and the hayloft above the stable.

It was here he saw the dried blood turned black and followed it to a crude ladder and saw the bloodied smears of a hand that had gripped the side. He climbed up softly to a small attic room high in the roof beams. It had been fitted out as a sleeping place for anyone having to care for a sick horse or await the birth of a foal. There on a narrow palliasse, lay a boy of twelve. He looked small for his years, pinched of face and unconscious. He had lost a lot of blood but he was alive.

Tumbleweed bent over him and examined the wound in his shoulder. The slug had gone straight through and out the other side. The palliasse was soaked in blood and if the boy died it would be because he'd bled to death.

Working swiftly he cleaned the wound with water from a tin pitcher and then plugged both holes with wads of cotton torn from one of the boy's shirts.

Tumbleweed looked about for a mug to give the boy a drink and then realized that he would eat with his grandmother. He only slept in the cosy little attic that held pegs for his clothes and little else except for a cross above the bed.

The boy's eyes fluttered open.

'Water ... I want water,' he whispered and his tongue moved about parched lips.

'That's all right, son. I'll get you water.'

'Who ... who are you? Are you with...?' and his voice trailed away.

'No. If you're talking about Cherrill, I'm hunting him. I'm a friend of Maria's...' He saw the relief in the boy's eyes. Then the eyes welled over and the boy cried softly and helplessly.

'You have a good cry, boy, it will do you good,' Tumbleweed said gruffly. 'I'm going to find you water and I'm going to bring you some beef stock. Now, stick it out, boy, until I come back.'

Tumbleweed was spooning beef stock into Roberto rather clumsily when Maria returned. He heard her shouting in the yard and seeing wooden shutters in the roof he opened them and looked down at her. He saw her panic at once.

'It's all right, Maria, Roberto's up here. He's shot and I'm feeding him soup. Can you get yourself up here?'

Maria took the ladder at a run. Her head, all covered in hay and dust, appeared. She was gasping and Tumbleweed thought he'd never seen her more beautiful or womanly as she gazed at Roberto. There was sure another side to this woman and he loved it.

'Oh, Roberto, what has he done to you?' She stroked his hair and kissed him on the mouth. 'It was Cherrill, wasn't it? There was no one else here to meet him?'

Roberto shook his head.

'Only Cherrill, Miss Maria. I heard an argument and shots and then Cherrill came and took two horses and the medicine man's wagon went hell for leather away from the ranch. I ran up to see what was happening. I saw Grandmother Carmen...' Roberto turned his face to the wall.

'Yes, Roberto, and then...?'

'I ran away when Cherrill started firing again. I felt something burn me and I forced myself to come to the attic. I could hardly climb the ladder...'

'But you did! You're very brave, Roberto. You're all I have left. Now we'll try and move you.'

'No!' Tumbleweed interrupted. 'We must leave him here for a while. It could be dangerous to move him. He's lost a lot of blood.'

Maria did not answer but removed the now soaking pads and slipped others into place. Then she looked at Tumbleweed.

'He needs more help than we can give him. Cochicata will send old Moonflower to tend him if we ask him. She carries herbs and simples and is very wise. She will look after him.'

Tumbleweed was packing both their saddle-bags with whatever he could find that would be useful on the long trek after Cherrill. He did not altogether trust the Mescaleros to find Cherrill before he moved out of their territory and so he was ready to follow on to land's end if need be, but get him he would.

He turned swiftly as a movement at the corner of his eye warned him of another presence. The presence stank of buffalo fat. A young buck with one feather tucked in a rawhide band around his forehead regarded him doubtfully. He gestured.

'Me Running Deer, you?'

'Tumbleweed.'

Running Deer's face relaxed into a half smile.

'You too, have Indian blood? Tumbleweed is not name I should like.'

Tumbleweed laughed. 'I am all paleface. I'm a drifter, so...' And his hands tumbled over each other as the tumbleweed did when the wind blew.

The youth nodded.

'I understand. No home, no roots. I come from Cochicata. He see signal and send out bucks. Now he want to know who we hunt!'

'Is he far from here?'

'No, he and his hand-picked wardogs are up in the hills. Already we hold the old man and his wagon for his protection. We have also picked up three riders coming into this land. They say they are looking for a man. Might it be the man we are also seeking?'

'Come into the house and you can talk to Miss Sanchez.'

'Maria? Of course. She is my cousin. It would be good to see her again.' Then he looked at Tumbleweed and went on shrewdly, 'Is it Maria's man we hunt?'

Tumbleweed nodded without answering but led the way from the corral to the ranchhouse, there to watch Maria squeal with pleasure and fling her arms about the stoical young buck who could not quite hide his delight at seeing her again.

139

Later Running Deer returned to Cochicata with news that Moonflower's services were required for Roberto and that man they were hunting was indeed Maria's man who had never been accepted by the Indians who had come in contact with him in the past.

A runner was sent to bring in Pig Whistle and his wagon. He would be needed to remove Roberto to the Indian village when Moonflower decided that he was well enough to endure the jolting of the clumsy unsprung wagon.

At last Tumbleweed and Maria could move out and lure Cherrill into the open if he indeed was still within a hundred mile radius of Mescalero territory. He was proving difficult to locate. Tumbleweed wanted in particular to talk to the three prisoners Cochicata held in a temporary camp. He had a sneaking feeling that Cochicata was going to lose face if Cherrill could not be found. His own humiliation would be passed on as a punishment to his bucks, and the three prisoners, if they would not talk, would suffer.

They could be innocent and looking for another man, but it seemed significant that they should turn up out of the blue at this time.

Cochicata greeted them with reserve. His loyalty to Maria was plain to be seen, but there was shame and anger in him, that he could not redeem his pledge of fealty when needed by producing the man they wanted. He was ashamed of his bucks for it reflected on their skills as trackers. The man, Cherrill, had disappeared into thin air.

So it was with reluctance that he allowed Tumbleweed access to the three white men held under guard in a buffalo skin tepee in the midst of the makeshift camp.

Tumbleweed knew what was in the chief's mind. If Tumbleweed was successful in making these men talk, then Cochicata's medicine was all wrong.

'Chief, I need your help,' he said diplomatically. 'I need you to sort truth from lies like sorting colts from fillies in roundup time. You understand? You will watch their eyes for lies. You are a great chief and wise in such things. I am but a drifter so you must help me.'

Cochicata's thin mouth relaxed and he nodded with great dignity.

'I watch and listen,' he said majestically, and Tumbleweed grinned inwardly. It was easy when you knew how the red man's mind worked!

141

He was glad the tall sinewy Indian was with him when he ducked his head and entered the stifling wigwam. None of the men who lounged on buffalo hides was shackled in any way. At least Cochicata was treating them well up until now.

Tumbleweed saw before him a tall Swede with a bushy blond beard. He'd met such men before. They drifted away from the gold fields when they grubbed up a stake and lit out usually looking for the ideal place to settle down. This one was cross-eyed and he had a nasty scar right across his forehead. A dirty fighter, Tumbleweed reckoned.

The second man was small and running to a beer belly. He didn't look anything special until one looked down and saw the empty holster strapped low on his leg and Tumbleweed realized he was looking at a professional gunman, a bounty-hunter, maybe?

The third man wore new levis, a leather jerkin over a checked shirt that wasn't more than a week into dirt. Now he could be a sheriff. He also wore two crossed belts with empty holster.

They all stared at him and then at the silent Indian who stood with arms crossed and a nasty look on his face.

'Well now, who have we here?' said the

well-dressed guy and the others laughed with that sycophantic hollow sound of men who laughed when there was nothing to laugh about. So Dandy here was the boss.

'I'm the one to ask the questions, mister. Just who are you and who're the arse-lickers with you?'

There was a growl from the others but Dandy only smiled.

'You noticed, eh? They're good at their job,' and he guffawed; then his face tightened. 'Tell that graven totem pole yonder that he has no right to hold us. It's a free country and we were harming no one. All we want to do is get on with our own business. Now you as a white man can understand and you can tell him our rights in all this.'

'Just what is your business, mister?'

'Why should I tell you? Let's just say I have an arrangement to meet someone...'

'Someone who owes you?'

The dandy's face flickered with surprise and the little paunchy character choked and covered it up by spitting on the ground. The Swede bunched fists like battering rams and suddenly Cochicata came alive and the Swede relaxed.

'What d'yer mean, owes me? Doesn't everyone owe someone something? We've got a deal on that's all.'

'What? Out in the middle of nowhere? Or are you on the rustling prod? You're way out of the cattle stations around here.'

Suddenly Tumbleweed's spine prickled. An idea had come out of the air and the thought was making him reel inwardly. His eyes narrowed.

'There's the Bisset Cattle Corporation just over the border. Is your business anything to do with William Bisset?'

'No ... no...' the Swede broke in before Dandy could speak. 'We haf no dealings with heem. We not give gob of spit to heem, even if he beg for it!'

'Shut up, you big bone-headed fool!'

'But boss...' the Swede was about to protest.

'For Chrissake, just stow it, will you?'

'So you all know Mr Bisset? Maybe you know my friend, Ted Ramsey?'

Suddenly there was a dead silence and it lasted around a minute and then the little paunchy feller said, 'By cripes! It's just like him to make other arrangements. Hey, mister, you're not here instead of him, are you?'

For a moment Tumbleweed's head whirled. The name had popped out for no more apparent reason than that Ramsey was never very far away from his thoughts. He also had a ranch running alongside the Bisset ranch and the two facts had tied in with each other.

'I could be. I'm also looking for a man called Cherrill...' and then stopped as Dandy gave a shout of laughter but the amusement in it was grim. He held up a hand.

'Hold your horses, boys. This feller ain't what he says he is or he'd know about Cherrill.'

'What about Cherrill?' Tumbleweed's voice was sharp.

'Hell! If you don't know, you're not one of Ramsey's pals. So it's no business of yours!' Dandy turned to the Swede and shook his head. 'And you, big face, keep hold of that tongue!'

Tumbleweed sprang forward and collared Dandy by the throat twisting his neckerchief as he did so and as Dandy clawed at his hands, his eyes started to bulge.

'You'll tell me what I want to know, damn you, or else I'll twist your head off your shoulders!'

The Swede lunged forward and the little man reached for a gun that wasn't there and suddenly the Indian chopped the Swede on the back of the neck and was using him as a battering ram to splatter the little man into the earth.

Grinning, he watched Tumbleweed with Dandy who was now turning blue.

'You want me to put them over a slow fire? I get truth without effort. Not like you who risk own life.'

Tumbleweed dropped the unconscious man and put a hand on Cochicata's shoulder.

'You great warrior and use head, but there is no need for slow burn. We get at truth this way. You see.'

Cochicata nodded.

'White man wise in some things, not others. I watch.'

Tumbleweed pulled the little man from under the Swede. He was gasping for breath and shit-scared.

'Look, mister, I only know what I was told. I'm only a hitman. I shoot when I'm told to and I don't ask the reason. I just hold my hand out for the pay. Now that's the truth and I swear it on my old mother's Bible, if she had one!'

'What's this about Cherrill?'

The little man licked his lips and his eyes rolled from one man to the other.

'They'll kill me if I tell you.'

'I'll kill you personal, if you don't!'

'Gee, mister, you make it hard for a feller. I want no trouble. Ramsey owes me and all I want is to catch up with him and get paid and then I'll light out for foreign parts. I want no truck with what comes after.'

'Then where does Cherrill come in?'

'Cherrill *is* Ramsey! Hell, now I've been and gone and done it! Ramsey doesn't want for folk to know. He's now respectable like and what happened during the war well-nigh forgotten. But for us who helped in his sideline of rustling ... well, he don't want Cherrill rampaging around no more, see?'

'And what makes you feel so safe? And why were you brought along?'

'I ... I...' Then the little man swallowed, and Tumbleweed watched realization come to him. He turned to the two men lying unconscious. 'By cripes, if I thought them two was bringing me along to murder me in cold blood I'd kill the bastards now!'

'Well, your guess is as good as mine, feller. Figure it out for yourself. Thanks for the information anyway.' He jerked his head at Cochicata and they both left the tepee.

Outside, Tumbleweed's head whirled. Cherrill was Ramsey. He couldn't believe how close he had been to his enemy! And Maria, she had been the murdering bastard's lover! That hurt more than having an arrow pulled out of his chest.

It was like acid burning in his stomach. He turned to Cochicata.

'String 'em up. Now it's your turn to play!'

Cochicata gave him a wide smile.

'Now paleface think like Indian. We make talk and get to know all truth!'

So Tumbleweed listened and observed the ways of the Indian with his enemies. Maria was held, protestingly, in the ranch-house. This was not women's business, nor was it his as time passed, and first the big Swede cracked followed closely by the little paunchy man who was looking decidedly thinner. Tumbleweed had protested that he had talked but Cochicata was adamant. He must not be judged as being merciful or he would lose the respect of his bucks.

The dandy died. He endured the fire and the red-hot iron bars and the castrating and at the end, the bucks were silent. This was a real man, even if he was a paleface. He would be buried with ritual.

So Ramsey is hanging around these parts to meet up with his three pals, is he? Tumbleweed ruminated. He's also found a

148

place to hide that the Indians can't find. Now where would that be?

His thoughts made him oblivious to his surroundings and Cochicata, glancing at him from time to time, wondered whether this white man could prove to be Maria's soulmate. If so, now that their benefactor, Eduardo Sanchez, was dead, then this man was the one to please.

'Your thoughts trouble you, Tumbleweed? You do not like what we do?'

Tumbleweed shrugged and made a brief gesture of denial with his hand.

'Your ways are perhaps not my ways, Chief, but who am I to judge? My mind troubles me because your bucks and dog soldiers have not found Cherrill. He is no shaman, so he could not fly away but your excellent trackers have not found him. I wonder where he could hide away? You know every cave, every hiding place in your territory, how is it he cannot be found?'

Cochicata stared sullenly ahead.

'Do you think one of my bucks has been bribed to let him slip through the net? None are reported missing, so the other alterative is that one of my trackers is not as good as we think he is. Is that what you are saying?'

'Hell, no, Chief! Far from it. I think he's

149

holed up because he knows he can't get through. Also that he was deliberately waiting for those three men. Only the dead man knew the real location. The other two are just gunslingers to obey orders. Now where do you suppose he would make his meeting point?'

Cochcicata suddenly came alive.

'Meeting point! The only place my bucks would not go would be the ritual ground opposite Needle Point. It was a sacred place and it is forbidden to go there unless the moon is full. We never go there in daylight. It is hallowed at the full moon but at any other time the place is accursed.'

'The ritual ground. What is that exactly?'

'A place of worship and sacrifice and where our medicine man can meditate and work as an oracle. There is a cave...'

'Ah, now that's better. I bet you the finest mare to a bag of horse shoe nails that that's the place to find him.'

'If it is so, none of my bucks will flush him out.' Cochicata spoke firmly. 'There is a spring within the cave. It is only a trickle but it would keep him alive for several days. Otherwise we must wait to starve him out.'

'Too long to wait. I'll go in myself and take him.'

'He would shoot you down before your eyes got used to the gloom.'

'Then I shall dress in the dandy's clothes and take the two prisoners and wait for him to come to us as must have been arranged.'

Cochicata nodded vigorously.

'Yes, I like it. Very cunning like red man would figure. Yes, we surround Needle Point and watch and wait. You will take him but if he should prove more skilful than yourself, then we shall avenge your death and Maria Sanchez' honour.'

'I want him alive. I mean to take him back to San Paulo and expose him for what he is, and then' – Tumbleweed exposed his teeth in a wolfish grin – 'I have business of my own to clear up.'

'You knew this man before?'

'Nope!'

'Then why...?'

Tumbleweed's jaw hardened.

'I was married for six months. My wife lived with my parents and my brother when I joined the Confederates. I was away for three years. After the war was over it took me six months before I returned to the farm. I had been wounded and lay a long time in military hospital. As I neared home, I found that I was travelling in the wake of a

151

marauding gang of ex-soldiers ... part of Quantrill's regiment. Quantrill himself was dead and one of his young lieutenants had taken over. I followed a trail of looting and burning, but I was alone and could do nothing about it. I little realized that they would find my parents' farm. I was a young fool. I should have anticipated it and got ahead of them. I rode behind thinking to save myself. It was the greatest mistake of my life.'

'And this man we hunt was him?'

'Yes. He passed himself off to Maria as Lee Cherrill and became a rustler, road agent and bank robber to finance his new life as Ted Ramsey. At least that's the way I see it for Ted Ramsey is one of the ranchers who is financing the banker Shawcross.'

'So why does he risk his honour by robbing this white man Shawcross who is supposed to be his friend?'

Tumbleweed shrugged.

'Maybe he needs money. The last two years' drought hasn't helped the cattle industry and rustling might not be so easy. Maybe he is threatened with exposure. He made mighty sure that those who could identify him were dead. That's why he wanted Maria killed. Who knows what a killer like him thinks and does?'

Cochicata's impassive glance rested on Tumbleweed's face.

'You will kill him?'

'Yes. It will avenge the past.'

'That is good. You will have cleansed your soul in blood and then there will be no aggression or hate in your heart. You will be born again.'

'If you say so, Chief, that will be so.'

'Then you will take Maria as your squaw?'

'Hey, now, don't go making plans. The little lady might not have marriage in mind.'

'I see it in her eyes. You will have to change your name,' and Cochicata gave the ghost of a smile.

'I think we'll have to find him first before we think of the future.'

Cochicata nodded and then left the fire and strode away into the darkness and a little later, Tumbleweed heard the soft call of a night owl. He knew Cochicata was calling in his bucks for a pow-wow.

Then he was back.

'We ride out an hour before dawn. You and the two prisoners will go now. You will take the main trail and ride down into the valley and stop at the north side of the Needle Point. You will see that behind you are the

Seven Sister hills. There is a butte jutting out from the middle Sister. It is flat-topped and the place we rally the dog soldiers for war and make our sacrifices to the full moon. Below, is a series of small caves hewn out thousands of years ago for worshippers to spend the night in shelter. Each one is just big enough for one man. But there is one which is a natural cave. It is halfway up the butte and can only be reached from one side. There is a path and this white man must have taken refuge there for that is one place our braves would not dare to search.' He looked at the night sky and said abruptly, 'You must go now; too much time has been wasted in pow-wow and soon the new day will begin.'

He rose in one fluid movement which Tumbleweed envied and stalked away. Soon, two young bucks appeared like magic at Tumbleweed's side.

'We are here because we talk good paleface talk and because we guard the two white men. We shall guide you through unknown trail to edge of plain and then you will proceed alone with prisoners but we shall follow, so that man you seek will expect only own men.'

'And Cochicata's other braves?'

The older of the two bucks smiled.

'They will be close by, above or below ground. The young men like to practise their merging with the nature spirits, so that they become invisible. Most are adept. Some young ones need more practice.' His teeth showed in a pleased grin.

'Oh!' So they merged with the so-called nature spirits, did they? mused Tumbleweed. No wonder the Mescalero Apache was respected in battle! 'So we go now?'

The Indian nodded. 'It is time.'

Quickly Tumbleweed dressed in the dead man's clothes. He was ready.

Three horses were being led from a makeshift corral and Tumbleweed saw that they were the white men's horses with all their trappings which was good. Along with them were the two bewildered white men.

'What goes on?' shivered the little paunchy feller who was sweating profusely. He'd heard of the nasty habit Indians had of tying a feller between two horses and tearing him apart...

'Nothing you might fear,' Tumbleweed grunted. 'We're going to ride out and meet Ramsey at the place appointed.'

'But we don't know anything! We can't tell...'

'We know. Maybe your ignorance might save your worthless lives! It all depends on you fellers. If you go quietly, then OK; if you don't...' He paused significantly and looked at the slim willow-whip Indians standing quietly by. 'You will find that they have their own favourite ways of treating their enemies!'

The men looked at each other and the big man nodded slightly and the little man turned back to Tumbleweed.

'We want no truck with Ramsey. We're just the hired help to see he got away. We're ready to sign on with you.'

Tumbleweed's lips curled in contempt.

'Feller, you sign on with nobody. You're already playing the part you're going to play. Savvy? Whether you like it or not! Now fork your horses and we'll ride.'

The little cavalcade moved out, the older Indian astride a blanket-covered mustang, going ahead, followed by the prisoners and Tumbleweed and the younger Indian flanking them and a little to the rear.

It was a silent bunch who moved forward at a cracking pace with the night wind blowing in their faces, for time was against them. Soon, dawn would be breaking and they needed to be riding over the flat plain alone so that Ramsey watching them high up on the Needle could follow their innocent seeming trail.

Tumbleweed knew in his bones that Cochicata was right. The only safe place in which to hide from the Indians would be in the heart of that rearing rock called Needle Point. For to the Indians it was a sacred place to be only approached with awe and reverence.

But if they played their cards right then Ramsey would come out and meet his men.

Tumbleweed smiled grimly in the dark. He would give his right arm to see Ramsey's expression when he saw the third member's face and realized that he was betrayed into coming down from his perch. He would give his other arm to witness Ramsey's terror when it was made known to him that he was the husband of the woman he'd raped and tortured before killing her and his family in that far-off secluded little ranch...

The leading Indian pulled up, rousing Tumbleweed from way-back thoughts that still gave him nightmares on occasion which he drowned in rotgut whiskey... But now he didn't need whiskey, he only needed revenge and it was only an ace away...

The horses bunched together. The Indian did not speak. He didn't need to. Tumbleweed knew the drill. His arm lifted in a salute and they were alone.

'Where the ... what the hell's happening now?' spluttered the little fat man. 'They're not letting us go?' There was hope and incredulity in his tone.

'Nope. You go along with me. It's coming up daylight and we ride on as if nothing was happening behind or at either side of us. Savvy? We're being watched, feller, don't forget it.' He looked at the silent Swede. 'The first hint of trouble, then you'll see just how close these Indians trail us and you never see 'em until they're on top of you! Now you' – nodding at the Swede – 'ride in front and we'll be right behind you; no looking around or acting up scared. Just be natural.'

Slowly they moved ahead and now it was a gradual descent to the valley floor. It gave the horses time to regain their wind. It also eased the riders.

But now there was no time for reflection. Tumbleweed gazed ahead as yet too far away, and the darkness just lifting. His body was tired, yet his mind was clear and the knowledge that he was close at last to the man he had hunted for six years sustained him. He wondered how long it would take Cochicata to organize his bucks into a blockade to prevent Ramsey from doubling back if he should smell a rat, up in the caves and tunnels of the Needle Point...

He looked down at himself. He was sure there was nothing to betray him that he was not the man Ramsey expected. He pulled the dandy's hat farther down over his face. He should pass muster at a distance.

The light grew stronger and the first yellowish-pink rays of the sun streamed across the distant hills. The horses reared their heads, eager to get into their normal easy canter, so they pranced and pulled and the Swede opened his mouth and cursed in thick guttural Swedish, and Tumbleweed guessed he didn't speak much English and relied on his little partner to get by.

Then suddenly all thought was washed from Tumbleweed's mind. Shock momentarily paralysed him and then his nerves prickled up and down his spine, galvanizing him into action. Something was wrong. Pig Whistle and his wagon were on a runaway track and fast closing the distance between them!

'Come on,' he bellowed, 'let's see what's wrong.' Without more ado he raked his horse's ribs and leapt ahead.

The little fat feller grinned up at his partner.

'Should we make a run for it?'

The big Swede looked about him and silently pointed. Behind them and all around them several heads appeared and in front a bold figure rose up with bow taut and an arrow ready poised to fly at its target.

The little man swallowed and scratched a bristly chin.

'I get the drift. It looks as if that feller wasn't giving us no bullshit. We'd better follow on, pard, and take a looksee why a medicine man should try his best to turn his wagon over.'

The Indian with the drawn bow allowed them to pass and then he merged into the undergrowth along with the rest of the braves.

They followed cheerfully behind. This was child's play and very amusing. It made a change to hunting and at the end of the day, there just might be the added attraction of seeing just how tough these white men were...

SEVEN

Maria looked at the small Indian boy with excitement tinged with apprehension. She watched him eat the plate of stew with an eagerness that was akin to starvation.

'You're sure about what you've told me, Little Beaver? You're not making it up so that I should feed you?'

The small boy looked at her solemnly with beady black eyes.

'You are a half cousin of my mother. I have heard it many times. She is proud to be of your blood. Would I lie to you?'

Maria shrugged. 'You might if you have run away from home and are starving. When did you eat last?'

'Two days ago. I was looking after my father and brother's horses and they broke their running ropes and galloped away. I ran as fast as I could after them. I followed for hours. I cannot go back without them. That is why I have come to you. Will you tell your men to look out for them? My father and brother will be very angry if I don't bring

161

them in.'

'They don't know of your loss?'

'Not yet.' The boy looked shame-faced. 'I am frightened to go home. They will beat me and the boys in the village will call me names for losing them. I will be shamed.'

'You do not know what has happened here?'

The boy shook his head.

'I have talked to no one. As I told you, I have only seen a white man hunting near Needle Point and he was too far away for me to ask about seeing six horses grazing anywhere.'

'It is just as well you were too far off! He might have shot you.'

The boy looked surprised. He paused in the gulping of his stew.

'Shot me? Why should he do that? We are friendly with all white men.'

'Not this one, you are not. He's dangerous and even now Cochicata and your father and brother and the other braves are out looking for him.'

'But how do you know it is the man Cochicata is looking for?'

'Little fool! How many strangers come into this valley? Very few people know this valley exists high up in the mountains. So he must be the man called Lee Cherrill. You have heard the name before?'

The boy nodded.

'I have heard my brother speak of him. He said...' Then he looked uncomfortable. 'I had not better tell you what he said.'

'I can guess.' And now Maria sounded bitter. 'If only I could get to him...'

'I could take you to him. I watched where he went. There is a trail at the back of Needle Point which climbs steeply. It is a narrow path like that made by goats. I think it is a private way up to the main cave and was used by the shamans so that they could appear as if by magic on the top of the butte, so I have heard my father say. It is a steep goat track but it could be climbed.'

'Then you will take me there!' Now Maria's eyes burned with determination. 'I shall take Pig Whistle. He can drive me in his wagon and you can ride too. What do you say?'

'If you will help me to find our horses afterwards?'

'Yes ... yes ... anything you say, but I want to find Lee Cherrill before Cochicata or the white man Tumbleweed finds him.' She bared her teeth which reminded Little Beaver of a she-wolf. 'Eat your food, fill your belly, for we shall soon be moving out!' And she strode away, her head filled with plans.

She found Pig Whistle snoring in her grandfather's rocking chair on the veranda and rocked it viciously until Pig Whistle fell on the floor.

'Get up, you drunken old sot!'

'What the hell's got into you, lady?' Pig Whistle scrambled up painfully. His old joints creaked most times but now after falling heavily, he was both winded and pained. He rubbed his knees with gnarled hands and looked decidedly sulky. 'What's a body to do round here but sleep?' he grumbled.

'Not in my grandfather's chair, you can't! Anyhow we're moving out so get those horses harnessed up. We're going after Lee Cherrill!'

'Eh? You must be loco, or are you joshing me because you found me sleeping in your old man's rocker?'

'No joshing, Pig Whistle. If you won't go with me, I'll harness up and take your wagon myself.'

'You damn well won't! No one drives those mules but me, they're my kids. Anyhow, they wouldn't budge for you. They're stubborn buggers, is them there mules, so that's it. You stay put. That there Tumbleweed feller said I was to look after you and I'm doing it here!'

'You're bloody well not! You and me's going to Needle Point and I'm going to kill that bastard before Cochicata or Tumbleweed get hold of him. I said I would kill him and I'm going to do just that!'

'You're mad, stark raving mad! He'll shoot you before you get within a hundred yards of him!'

'Oh, no he won't.'

'How can you be so damn sure?'

'Because I'll strip. He'll think all's forgiven and he'll be hungry for a woman, you'll see.'

Pig Whistle's eyes bugged.

It was a long time since he'd seen a woman naked, never mind having one. He licked his lips. It would be worth the risk of taking her...

'You really mean that? You would strip for him?'

'Yes, why not? I've done it often before. He's seen it all.' She sounded bitter. 'But there'll be a difference.'

'And what will that be if I might ask?'

Her eyes flashed.

'You mind your own business, old man, and go get that wagon harnessed up!'

'I'm damned if I will! If you treat me like dirt, then to hell with you!'

'Then hell it'll be!' Suddenly he was staring down at a little snub-nosed pistol that

165

fitted snugly in her hand. She smiled coldly at the look in his eyes. 'I'm not joshing you, Pig Whistle, I mean it. There's been plenty death around here: another stiff won't make much difference. Now then, what's it to be?'

'But why the wagon? Why not go on horseback?' he croaked.

'I can't take what I want to take on horseback. Besides, there's the Indian boy. He knows a way up that Needle and he goes with us.' She jerked the weapon and Pig Whistle's eyes closed and sweat broke out on him causing her to wrinkle her nose. 'Get moving pronto or...'

He shuddered and moved fast. Hell! There was no telling what a woman would do when she was worked up enough and by golly, she was worked up enough to explode!

The long afternoon turned to night and though weary, Maria sat with back straight and the same determination in her as at the outset. Little Beaver crouched in the back amidst the ironware, the sacks of coffee, the dried goods and all the items on offer to ranch wives who never made the journey to the nearest town.

She could stand the lumbering sway of the wagon, the spine-jolting torture but sitting next to Pig Whistle turned her physically sick so she concentrated on her hatred for Lee Cherrill and what she should do when they met.

The box at her back reassured her. At first, Pig Whistle had objected to carrying it, but waving her little friend, the pocket derringer, had persuaded him.

Now she concentrated on her plan.

She had changed to heavy snuff-coloured skirt and a low-cut blouse of the type that he would respond to. He loved to see a hint of breast, the promise of what was to come later.

She would climb Needle Point as stealthily as any old shaman and come upon him unawares. She would send the boy away when he had shown her the path.

Then she would take her time, taunt Lee about what he was missing ... show him ... stir up his juices and then...

Her mouth curved in a smile of anticipation. She would show him that no one could steal her love and betray her, and live! She would take one of his small black cigars which he knew she liked and then, when he was relaxed she would take from under her skirt as she pretended to slip it off, the sticks of dynamite.

They would die together.

And she was glad of it.

She hurt inside so much at the loss of her grandfather and those she knew that death beside that beast was the only solution. She was alone in the world, except for the token allegiance to the Mescaleros. And as for the man, Tumbleweed, she could have loved him but there was some instinct in her that said he would always be restless, a rover, a man looking over the next horizon.

She didn't want a man who could not settle on that secluded mountain ranch. Better that it should revert to Indians.

Her gloomy reverie was broken by the mules nickering nervously and then their plunging brought Pig Whistle hauling savagely on the reins.

'What in hell's the matter with you both?' he yelled in exasperation. 'God damn it! They're as nervous as if they'd seen a mountain cat!'

'What is it, Pig Whistle? There must be something out there.' She peered out from the wagon awning into the blackness of thick undergrowth because they were on the verge of the plain.

'How the hell do I know? But the mules are sure jumpy!'

Suddenly there was the click of a rifle

being cocked and Maria's spine froze. At the same time Little Beaver struggled awake and sat up bemused.

'What's happening?'

'Shh, someone's out there.'

Then a raucous voice hailed the wagon. 'Ho there, whoever you are, come out and come out peaceful!'

Pig Whistle swore under his breath and eased himself creakingly to the ground. Maria put out a warning hand to stop Little Beaver from moving and then quietly and gracefully stepped down.

A flare of light from a lucifer dazzled them both and then the laugh that Maria knew well came on the night air.

'Well, well! If it isn't the lovely Maria! And what might a flower like you be doing in this wilderness? You should be tucked up in bed ... with a lover perhaps!'

Maria bunched her fists. This wasn't going as she planned it. She was the one who should have been on top, dishing out the wisecracks, hurting him...

He came nearer, his rifle still pointing significantly at them both. His glance at Pig Whistle was cursory but it was enough to paralyse the old man.

'I don't like your choice in men, Maria. I

think you're slipping.' He grinned at her and then grimaced as the lucifer burned his fingers.

He ducked as her hand came up to slap his face but he caught her wrist.

'Still the same fiery Maria! How about a kiss for old time's sake and then you can tell me why you're here? Is it the bank roll?'

He laughed as he pulled her to him and his kiss was still as exciting as ever as he explored her mouth with that old familiarity which started a churning low down in her gut.

Then she managed to struggle free.

'I'm not your Maria any more, Lee.' She rubbed her mouth with her hand. He frowned.

'No? I think you are. In fact I know you are. You're my woman until I tire of you.' He laughed again in pure amusement. 'Don't you know your body tells me you're a woman? You can't resist me, Maria.'

'Yes I can, Lee.' But she knew she was lying. Once in his arms the old fire would be lit. She knew it and, damn it, he knew it only too well!

She did not answer and he shook her none too gently, and then swept the long silky hair out of her eyes.

'Maria, whatever you say, you came

looking for me, didn't you?' His voice was low and caressing. She shivered and he mistook the shiver and he smiled triumphantly in the darkness.

Then he was suddenly aware of the old man standing close by. The smell offended his nostrils and an ungovernable rage overcame him to think that she would give herself to this revolting old man!

The rifle butt cracked down on Pig Whistle's unprotected head and he fell to the ground before he knew what was happening.

Maria stared with horror. She'd never seen the violent side of Lee. He had always seen to it that other men did his business and now she was appalled.

'Lee, you've killed him!'

'No way. He's a tough old nut. He'll live and if he doesn't, who cares?' Then he was staggering back as the Indian boy leapt from the wagon and his weight knocked Lee Cherrill to the ground. He wielded a knife aiming for Cherrill's heart but the man was too strong and his reflexes too quick for the boy. The knife drew blood but did not penetrate and then Cherrill rolled free and viciously clubbed the boy over the head.

Breathing hard, he got to his feet before Maria could think of moving. Grabbing her, he aimed a blow at her chin. Blackness swooped down on her and he caught her as she fell.

She was a light weight and slinging her over his shoulder, he recovered the two jackrabbits he'd snared and come back for and loped off, Indianwise, to climb the hidden trail up into his cave. At least he was going to have all the amusement and company he needed until those three accomplices turned up.

He would enjoy Maria until the time came when he must go back to the life of Ted Ramsey. Then ... his mind slurred over Maria's fate. There was always somebody who would do the dirty work for the right kind of money, and he had plenty of that right now. Yes, Maria was a godsend. Beautiful, passionate and in love with him. He could stay put forever if need be. He tackled the climb with gusto. He would have the rabbits cooked by the time she came round. They would eat and then they would make love and tomorrow would be another day...

The wagon came to a standstill. Pig Whistle looked ghastly and to Tumbleweed's surprise a small boy sat beside the old man. He too looked as if he had been beaten up.

'Hello there, what's all the rush?' Tumbleweed leaned forward and grabbed the near mule's bridle, making his own mount dance nervously. The mule's eyes rolled and foam drifted off a sweated neck as did its mate. 'You'll kill those mules if you always travel at that lick,' he said sharply. 'What brings you here?'

'It's Maria. The stupid bitch heard from this damned kid that Cherrill was up on Needle Point. She got the idea she could seduce him and kill him...'

'You mean you allowed her to come out here? Why you son of a bitch, I should kill you!' He leapt down from his horse and dragged Pig Whistle from his perch.

'For God's sake, feller, I had no option! She got the drop on me. I had to take her. She was like a madwoman. She would have killed me if I'd held out. Ask the kid, he'll tell you!'

Tumbleweed let him go and Pig Whistle rubbed his neck. It felt as if it had been jerked from his spine.

'Then where is she now?'

'That's why I was coming hell for leather to find you! Honest to God, I was...'

Tumbleweed grabbed him again and shook him.

173

'Stop pissing around. What's happened to her?'

Pig Whistle swallowed and then looked in the distance to the Needle now to be seen in the early dawn.

'She's up there with Cherrill. He got the drop on us and laid me out and the kid too. We must have been out for hours.'

'Jesus Christ! Of all the bloody foolhardy things to do and I told you to look after her! I should cut your liver out!'

'Look, as I said, I had to come. The kid was going to show her a way up Needle Point so that she could surprise him. She had this little pocket gun, you know, the ones the gamblers use...'

'Yes, yes, stop babbling you old fool and let me think.'

He turned to the two silent listeners, and made up his mind quickly.

'You fellers in with me on this?'

'Yeh, well we can't be otherwise what with Cochicata waiting to cut our balls off if we show fight,' the little fat man said judiciously. 'He does what I do,' indicating the Swede.

'Good. Then remember he's got the bank roll up there and I'm damned as to what happens to it. Savvy? Shawcross's loss doesn't worry me none. All I want is this bastard and I want him alive.'

'What about Cochicata and his boys going up there and taking him?'

'No dice. They'll not set foot on Needle Point. It would be desecration for them. You know what peculiar beliefs the Indians have for their own spirit places.'

The little man nodded.

'That figures. They'd rather die than go against their gods. What you think of the chances he'll leave the woman and come down and meet us?'

Tumbleweed shrugged.

'Depends how soon he finishes with Maria. It could take time. On the other hand if he's keen to make contact with us. He might tie her up, come down to make what arrangements he was going to make and expect to go fetch her.'

His jaw tautened as he thought of Maria with that bastard. Maybe even now he was putting her through an ordeal, or would it be an ordeal? His jaw clenched even more as another kind of jealousy knifed through him. She might be liking what was happening to her!

Then Pig Whistle jerked him back to the present.

'There's dynamite in that there box.'

Tumbleweed's head snapped up. 'Why didn't you say sooner?'

'Never thought of it. She was going to use it somehow.'

'My God, I'm glad she didn't have the chance. The fool woman would have killed herself in the process.'

'She would know the drill. Her grandfather used dynamite to clear tree stumps and blast boulders. She would know the danger all right.'

Tumbleweed stared at him.

'Are you saying she would have killed herself deliberately?'

'Something like that. She was mad enough all right. She was a really crazy loco, that woman was.'

'Jesus! She said she hated him, but I didn't realize just how deep it went. Then it can't be a good time up there for her. Now this is what we do...'

The mules and the wagon were driven farther into the lush undergrowth and tethered and Little Beaver was to run as fast as he could towards Needle Point keeping well under cover and if he should encounter any of his Indian friends then he should tell them what was happening and to stand back and not interfere – whatever happened in front of the Needle.

The boy nodded and slipped away and Tumbleweed and the two gunmen made their leisurely way down the valley in full view of anyone on the lookout for them. Tumbleweed rode a little way behind to make sure his disguise was not penetrated. He might dress in the dandy's clothes but he sure might not hold himself or ride like him. A suspicious discerning eye on the lookout for treachery might see him for a stranger.

They moved at a measured easy pace to give the impression all was well. Gradually they moved closer and could see the high wide mouth shadowed and sinister and Tumbleweed's spine tingled. They were being watched. He was sure of it.

They were now having trouble with the horses for they were being held on a tight rein and every now and then their rumps would rise as they bunched together.

'I wish he would get on with it,' the little fat man grumbled as nerves grew tight. 'He sure is a suspicious bastard...'

Then suddenly he coughed and choked and leaned forward before sliding from his horse, and a split second later came the report of the rifle. The horses reared and again came a report and the big Swede crashed into the ground, the horse galloping off after the other.

Tumbleweed's swift reflex action was to drop to the ground Indian style and roll. He finished up cracking his spine against a boulder. But he was on his knees in a flash and hunkering behind the protection that the boulder gave. He cursed. Some thing had given them away but he didn't know what ... unless it was because dandyboy had been the leader and would never have ridden behind the gunmen.

He cursed again. He was no mind doctor to figure out a man's reasoning. He was just a plain, good, old-fashioned ex-soldier who obeyed orders, used his rifle and his Colt to survive and until now minded his own business with one idea in mind ... to get Ted Ramsey. After that, his future to him had always been vague. He never had been able to envisage life without that one all-powerful goal.

But now the time was in the here and now. Six years of hunting were nearly over, and he would confront the man who killed his family. But he never envisaged for one moment that a woman would come between them. He cursed Maria again for interfering.

Two quick reports and the tell-tale puffs of

smoke showed where he was hiding. The bastard had him pinned down.

Then the faint drumbeats started, and they echoed up and down the valley. It was a pulsating sound that merged with a man's heartbeat. It was a sinister hypnotic call to a man's inner spirit. It called, stirred up emotions and sent tingles up a grown man's spine.

There was no doubt about it, Cochicata was sending out his own message to Ted Ramsey.

The drumbeats grew more urgent until they beat a tattoo in the head and Tumble-weed himself felt their power.

He snapped a shot to discover whether Ramsey was still out there watching or had returned to the cave. Tumbleweed was too near the high perpendicular rock to be able to see what was happening at the cave entrance.

Then Little Beaver was plucking at his sleeve.

'The white man has now gone inside the cave. Do you want me to show you the hidden trail now?' The boy's bright eyes looked enquiringly at him.

Tumbleweed nodded and the boy bellied back amongst the undergrowth and Tumbleweed followed. There, in the shelter of the rocks far to the left of the rearing butte was a small group of braves waiting for him.

Little Beaver led him to the oldest man amongst them.

'This is my father. I have already told him that you and the Senorita Sanchez will find our horses. That is so, isn't it?'

'Of course, anything you say, young 'un. You show me the way up that bloody rock and you can have anything you wish.'

Little Beaver's father looked grave and disapproving.

'I have told my son that he should not do this thing. It is bad medicine, but he is upset at losing our horses and thinks it is the Great Spirit's showing of the way he can atone. You will not allow my son to climb all the way? You will send him back before he reaches the sacred part of Needle Point?'

'Yes, I swear it by the honour of a pale face.'

'Huh! That is no good. Indians of all tribes know that white men do not always honour their promises. You promise on your own spirit! You take responsibility for own destiny if you fail!'

'I swear it on the well-being of my spirit. May I roam forever in the twilight world if I break my oath! Your boy will not tread on holy ground or come to harm, I promise you.'

The hook-nosed Indian nodded, satisfied.

'Success be yours, white man. I do not understand why this man should violate our sacred place but your honour will be our honour. The Great Spirit will be with you if your heart is white.' He turned to his son. 'Now you go and do what you have to do and return to us with a glad heart. The horses will not be lost, only roaming the valley. You have already been punished because you have already anticipated the jeers and laughter of your companions. That is enough. Now go.'

Tumbleweed followed carefully in the boy's footsteps and the way wound around the elaborate twisting path that took in all the protection of crevices and boulders until they came to a natural crack in the foot of the Needle and at the far side from the natural flat top where the shaman appeared as if by magic.

It was hard for a bulky man like Tumbleweed to ease himself through the crack but when he did so, he was surprised because the crack widened into a fair-sized cave. It was here the shamans and medicine men changed their everyday attire for something

181

more impressive because even now there were blankets and feathered headdresses hanging on iron hooks in the living rock.

Little Beaver reached upwards and found a twist of hemp soaked in buffalo fat which he lit with one of Tumbleweed's lucifers.

The dim light showed a rough hewn stairway just wide enough for a man to climb upwards. It looked to Tumbleweed like a natural cleft in the rock carved out over thousands of years by running water and utilized by enterprising medicine men for their own private purposes.

The way was rough and uneven. The steps were of uneven thickness as if someone had taken advantage of what was already there. Several times he stumbled and the air was thick with smoke and he began to worry that Ramsey would become alert to the fact someone was coming up to the cave by the back way.

They reached a second level and now the crack in the rock reached its outer edge and the torch was extinguished. It would be needed no more. The sun's glare blinded them for a moment and they stood and when they could look they saw the breathtaking view of the far distant Seven Sisters Hills and the hint of river and falls far far to the south.

The boy waited for Tumbleweed to begin the next part of the climb. Silently he pointed to a narrow ledge that wound away from this the last semblance of a cave.

'You mean, that's the way I go?'

The boy nodded. 'I must not go with you now. You are on hallowed ground. This is where I must leave you. Look, that trail joins what is farther along a goat trail. You follow it all the way to the top and you come out on the sacrificial ledge. From there, it is easy to get to the big cave. You understand?'

'Sounds easy, boy, if I was an antelope or a goat, but if the old men could climb it I suppose I can.'

'I will ask the Great Spirit to help you.'

'Thanks, boy. If I return, I'll not forget your help.'

'You will make sure our horses are returned? My father may be more angry than he tell you. He can speak with forked tongue,' and the boy showed his strong even teeth in a grin that stretched from one side of his face to the other.

Tumbleweed grinned back. He warmed to this kid. He had a good sense of humour.

'You'll have your horses even if I have to round them up myself!'

The boy raised his arm in a last salute and

183

then he turned and disappeared down the dark stairway like a young cat.

Tumbleweed contemplated the ledge. If Ramsey was on the prowl this would be a good time for Tumbleweed to be sent into oblivion with a touch of the hand. So it behoved him to get past that bad patch as soon as possible. Gritting his teeth he moved out on to the ledge and found that by edging one foot at a time he could move sideways and around the bend and, by jutting pieces of rough rock, he could get fairly good handholds. That gave him confidence, but he dared not look down. He was already at least thirty feet up from the boulders on the ground.

He was sweating hard when finally he reached the gradient and stepped on to firmer flatter ground. He saw then that the path which led upwards also led downwards and round past a block of granite that must have come to a full stop during some past ice age.

Cautiously he moved upwards and found that the path spiralled and continued upwards. Nothing stirred, not even a bird moved on that rocky path and so, panting and grabbing tufts of lichen to help him, he finally reached the top. He lay panting for several minutes before rising and exploring the large flat top of Needle Point. He stepped to the edge and looked down and then right along the valley from the direction they had come. It was windy and exhilarating and something in him made him reach for the sky with both hands.

It was then the faint beat of the drums became louder until they were crashing and rolling and echoing so that they pierced the very heart of those who heard it. He smiled.

It was Cochicata's response. He and his drummers were watching and the drumbeats sent their own messages just as the smoke fires did, but the drums played on the emotions whereas the smoke relayed actual talk.

The increased drumming brought another response. There was the scrape of boots, a cursing as Ramsey climbed a short stairway from the main cave, and Tumbleweed tensed, ready to fling himself on the unsuspecting man.

He waited for Ramsey to appear, his intention to shoot him in the shoulder. He didn't want to kill him ... not yet. He wanted him to suffer. He raised his Colt to take the aim and his finger stiffened on the trigger ready and waiting and then he drew breath and lowered the gun. Maria was being held in an armlock.

'You bitch!' Ramsey was muttering. 'I'll teach you to try and knife me! I'll hang you over that damned cliff and see how you like it! I'll have you begging for your life. You'll do anything I ask you to do! I'll make you pay as long as you live.'

'You don't frighten me, you bastard! Sanchez women don't frighten so easily. You killed my folks. I don't fear dying, but you'll go with me!' And she bit into the muscle at the top of his arm where it covered her neck. He yelped but hung on.

She didn't know how long she'd been lying in the big cave. The wind howled and gusted in the opening. She was lying on a blanket and her jaw ached. She opened her mouth and she moaned. At once she heard the scrape of feet on the uneven rock. He was hunkering down beside her.

'How're you feeling? Sorry I had to cold-cock you but it saved an argument. Want some stew? It's ready.'

She struggled to sit up, her brains felt like scrambled eggs.

'How long have I been out?'

'Long enough.'

'What about the boy and Pig Whistle?'

He shrugged. 'Hell! How should I know? I'm not their keepers. In fact I hope they never come round. Dirty old bastard! How could you go with him? You must be out of your mind, and as for the kid, he's only a stinking Indian!'

He stood up abruptly and walked away. Maria was conscious of the smell of stewed rabbit and her stomach cramped. He came back with a tin bowl that steamed and a spoon and a thick piece of cornbread.

'Here, eat this. It'll put some colour into your cheeks.'

It was hard chewing. The rabbits must have been old bucks and the lumps were hard to get down what with her bruised chin and all. She sopped her bread in the gravy and that was better. Then he offered her cool spring water that welled up at the back of the cave.

She looked about curiously. He'd lit a firebrand already placed in a bracket on the wall. It smoked and flared and cast a yellow-orange glow over the whole cave leaving the corners in shadow.

Under the firebrand a small stone fireplace had been erected but it was a primitive thing with only a spit for turning joints of meat. Above, the rock wall was blackened with smoke. This place had been the scene of many ceremonies, human sacrifices included.

She shuddered. There was an eeriness about the place that called to her Indian blood. She wanted to have done with this cat and mouse game. He was being his old self, helpful and charming except for the outburst about the boy and Pig Whistle. Away from him, her resolve was clear. She would kill him. But she knew that if he came to her demanding her body and he caressed her in that special way he had, she would surrender to him and hate herself afterwards.

He watched as she ate, his eyes hot for her. He was mentally stripping her and as his lips and tongue writhed she knew he was once again licking and sucking her nipples and she felt her nipples stiffen in response.

She glanced about her but there was no knife to be seen. She saw that he had a knife strapped to his waist. It was a broad Bowie knife used for hunting. If only she could get her hands on that!

Then he was taking her bowl away and drawing her to her feet and she felt his arms go about her and the quivering of his body. His breath was sour as he sought and found her lips. Then he was kissing her throat and the hollow of her neck and far away a horse whinnied and she felt the shock streak through him.

He muttered a curse and thrust her from him and as he did so she felt his arousal. Lee hated to be deprived. When he came back she knew he would be rough with her. He always had been.

'What is it?'

He did not answer but picked up his rifle, slid bullets into the breech and moved quietly outside and to the back of a jutting rock.

He looked down at three horsemen. He smiled in triumph and was in the act of coming out and waving to them when he paused. Something wasn't right. Jake Kingsley, who was in charge of his hired gunmen, never rode behind his men. Jake Kingsley was a very jealous man. He was very aware of any slight. He would never allow someone else to take the lead. If it wasn't Jake down there who was it? And why did the big Swede and little Willy act as if nothing was wrong?

The answer was clear. Jake was dead and those two gunslinging bastards had sold out to another boss. They were after his bank roll!

Cursing, he drew a bead on the little fat man and watched him bounce out of his saddle. Then he screwed up his eyes; the target was bigger this time. The Swede hadn't hit the ground before he triggered a shot at the third man. But he was too late. Whoever he was, was smart; he'd rolled clear and continued rolling until he was within a mess of rocks. Snapping off several shots he figured he had whoever was impersonating Jake sewn up. This could be a waiting game. From his vantage point he could see every move.

But the faint menacing drumbeats began and they got to him. They pounded in his head, stopping him figuring what to do next. The steady beat was sending him mad.

'Come on, you bastards,' he called hoarsely. 'You'll never get me up here no matter how long you wait!'

Laughing and muttering to himself and completely forgetting the strange third man he made his way back to Maria. He paused, watching her as she examined his bedroll and then his saddle-bags. So the bitch was after his bankroll.

He was trembling and it surprised him. It was the damned menace in those drumbeats. They were hypnotizing him, frightening him with their unspoken message. He felt like a cat whose fur was being rubbed the wrong way. It was so bad that he completely forgot the shootings and the man who got away.

He knew that the talking drums were connected with his takeover of the Indians' sacred place. He knew all the spirit stuff was a load of horse balls and yet some superstitious niggle at the back of his mind was growing into a huge black 'thing'. Fear turned into rage that aimed itself at Maria as the only human being near him.

He bounded across the cave floor and gripped her neck with one hand. The other was raised to strike.

'You bitch! So you're after the money! You're like all the rest, well let me tell you something, honey, you won't see a cent and that's flat!'

The blow across the face half-stunned her. She screamed and feebly struggled to free herself. He hit her again and fell with her on to the blanket. He kissed her forcefully, bruising her lips and hurting her already bruised jaw. The last vestiges of attraction for him left her. Her loathing enveloped her and made her skin crawl. How ever could she have regarded him with love? How could she, even those few hours past have been afraid that she might once again feel his animal attraction?

She drew on her last strength and lashed

out catching him in the eye before he captured her wrists together. The pain infuriated him further. He tore her blouse exposing the rounded breasts with the roseate nipples and watched their movement as she heaved and gasped for breath.

Then came the final assault. It was rape at its worst when he neither considered her or himself. He was just a beast obliterating his fear of the drums, drowning in sexual explosion and collapsed on top of her when it was over. His breath came in long shuddering gulps and he lay still.

Maria closed her eyes and prayed and suddenly remembered his knife at his waist. A stealthy movement and she was dragging it out of its sheath, but she was too clumsy and too late. As she turned it on him, his eyes opened wide with shocked incredulity.

Then he was springing to his feet and dragging her with him. His arm about her waist like a cruel vice. She fought him silently saving her breath for a final supreme effort.

He was muttering to himself and calling her whore and slut and trying to bite her neck and breasts. She knew she was fighting a ravening beast.

Then, he gave a low gurgling laugh and her blood ran cold.

'You're a cow and we all know what happens to cows. We kill 'em and quarter them and hang 'em up!' And he was dragging her up the short flight of stairs to the sacrificial ledge. 'If they want a sacrifice, I'll give 'em one! You bitch ... I'll teach you to knife me...'

Half-fainting she heard his words roll over her. Then she rallied, self preservation giving her a last surge of defiance.

'You don't frighten me you bastard! Sanchez women don't frighten easily. You killed my folks. I don't fear dying, but you'll go with me!' She ducked her head and bit the muscle at the top of his arm where it covered her neck. She heard him yell but hung on, but now her strength was almost gone. She hung on by sheer willpower and was fighting a blackness that was now overwhelming her.

She didn't know when she hit the ground.

EIGHT

'Drop her Ramsey! Or I'll part your hair and I can do it!'

Ted Ramsey was transfixed. The voice alone paralysed his reflexes. He dropped

193

Maria like a sack of corn and Tumbleweed steeled himself not to look at the pitiful bloodied half-clothed woman. Anger blazed in him but it was ice-cold controlled rage.

'Who ... who the hell are you? You're not a goddamn Indian.'

'I've come to take you in, Ramsey.'

'Why not just shoot me? I've no gun, only this knife.' He gestured at his side.

Tumbleweed's reflex was to raise his gun.

'No tricks, Ramsey. As you say, I could kill you like a rat but that isn't my style.'

Ramsey visibly straightened, suddenly more confident and now the drums were silent, his wits were working overtime.

'What is your style, mister? You want for us to share that bank roll? It's down there lying sweet and tempting. We could both get away if we take the woman. Cochicata's band won't harm us if we threaten to kill her. What about it?'

Tumbleweed's answer was a long slow chuckle and it had no amusement in it. It wiped the ingratiating smile from Ted Ramsey's face.

'What is it you do want, mister?'

'As I said, I'm committed to take Lee Cherrill, alias Ted Ramsey, one-time lieutenant to the renegade, Quantrill and now

194

very respectable rancher, with secret rustling connections, back to Shawcross, the banker, whom I'm sure has his own little problems of double-cross with the inhabitants of San Paulo. But they're not my concern. All I'm interested in is the bounty on your head. You're worth five hundred bucks to me, feller, and I'm hungry enough to collect!'

'Five hundred bucks? But that's chicken feed to what you would get if you pitch in with me. How does fifteen thousand sound to you?'

'So the bank roll was worth thirty thousand?'

'Yeh. I sat and counted it one night. Took most of the night.'

'And were your hands dirty afterwards?'

Ted Ramsey looked puzzled. 'I don't get your drift, mister.'

'No, you wouldn't. You wouldn't even recognize shit if you saw it. You would think it was what other folk ate! Now let's quit this talking business. There's something I want to do before I take you in.'

'What the hell's bugging you now, mister?'

'Well, let's say there's unfinished business going back years. You remember the little secluded ranch way back in the hills? I don't need to remind you just where it was located. You will be able to bring it to mind when I tell you that you rode in with six other men, all Quantrill's men, and supposed to be on army business. The men killed the livestock and took away meat and fodder and stripped the place of everything. You shot the rancher because he objected to what was going on. You shot his teenage son. Then finally ... you shot the rancher's wife for trying to protect her daughter-in-law from you.' Tumbleweed paused. This was hard, talking about this man's actions to his face. Emotion welled up in him turning his brain on fire. He wanted to rend and tear. 'You shot a Mexican who didn't die immediately, nor did my brother. They told me how you tortured my wife after you raped her, and when you were finished, you shot her like an animal. They both died in my arms in terrible pain,' he finished, with an icy calm that brought a chill to Ramsey's veins. His face turned white.

'They were lying! It's all a lie! There were others. I couldn't stop them. Quantrill's men were famous for meting out justice to traitors! They were trash...' Now Ramsey was sweating and babbling. 'Look, I've offered you half of what I've got. Come on, we can share and share alike.' His eyes lighted on the slumped body of Maria. 'You can even share the woman.'

Tumbleweed looked at him with loathing.

'You're worse than an animal, Ramsey! A yellow-streaked load of shit, whose soul is damned to hell! You're gonna rot, feller, real slow, and when I get through with you and take you back to San Paulo you'll be glad to see Shawcross and those townsfolk ... and after they're through with you, I'm going to kill you! For you haven't any balls to do anything about it!'

The deliberate prodding paid off. Tumbleweed tensed, for all the signs were there, the flickering eyes, the intention and when Ramsey's knife flew through the air, he ducked and lunged and caught Ramsey at the knees. They rolled away from Maria and then came the gouging and punching and kicking and they both fought with the experience of barroom brawls. Rolling and twisting and blood flying, Tumbleweed experienced an ecstasy that was all pain and exhilaration. He gloried in the deliberate punishment of Ramsey's most vulnerable parts. It was a vicious onslaught without mercy, each punch was for all his family and his wife, all with six years of added interest. Tumbleweed's knuckles stung. The punches at the kidneys, the gouging of the eyes, the groin, the kneecaps, the hand side edge punches at the throat. It went on and on, and Tumbleweed took a beating in the process.

Both men were staggering, their muscles failing when Tumbleweed summoned his last strength. He could see that Ramsey was becoming oblivious to any more punishment. His breath was coming in great rasping breaths that hurt his lungs. He was bleeding and one eye was entirely closed. They were two animals fighting to the death...

Tumbleweed drew back a fist that seemed too heavy to lift and managed the last head-jolting haymaker which lifted Ramsey high in the air and broke Tumbleweed's knuckles.

Ramsey came down with a crash and lay, one leg twitching, and finally becoming still.

Tumbleweed passed a trembling hand over his forehead, staggering a little and then he collapsed into a heap.

A resonant drum was beating his brains out when he recovered consciousness. He tried to rise but found himself in the cave and covered by a blanket.

Maria was bending over him trying to administer something that tasted nasty on his lips.

'What ... what happened? How did I get here?'

She smiled. She looked haggard and pale and the bruises showed but she was now cleaned up and wearing an old Indian jerkin. It smelled faintly of buffalo fat.

'Little Beaver braved the wrath of the Great Spirit and came up when everything went quiet and then he sent word to Cochicata who came at once with Pig Whistle. He has been very good. He gave me this leather jerkin and the ointment for your wounds and for mine and also this vile stuff which I assure you will clear your head as it did mine. Pig Whistle is an angel in disguise and he didn't mind scrambling up the rock. He said Indian spirits never scared him, only man-made spirits that conjure up pink snakes!'

'And what about, Cochicata?'

'He dared climb the Needle because he has a sacrifice in mind to cleanse Needle Point of Ramsey's violation.'

'A good idea. What has he in mind?'

'A sacrifice. A spilling of blood to appease the Great Spirit.'

She spoke matter of factly and he nodded and relaxed and ate some stewed rabbit. It was tough but it gave him a surge of new strength.

She sat and watched him and he could not read her mind.

Then, replete and taking a second cup of Pig Whistle's coffee, his mind began to work.

'What's all the drum business? It sounds like one drum and here on the rock, not like before when it sounded as if it echoed all round the hills. It's here on the rock, isn't it?'

'Yes. Cochicata is summoning all the tribe. It is going to be big medicine. Something that the children will talk about for years to come.'

'How you know all this?'

'You forget, I've got Indian blood and I'm now their patron. Cochicata deems it is his duty to inform me of what is going on just as he did with my grandfather. He says I should find a man to help and sustain me.'

Her eyelids fluttered and then lowered as she spoke.

'Maria...'

'Yes...?' She leaned nearer, suddenly eager to listen.

'I want to say...'

But he never got to say what he had in mind. He hadn't been quite sure himself. He was confused, still woozy... Cochicata stood in the cave entrance, a tall commanding figure dressed in full regalia of splendid feathered headdress and feathered cloak, his bare bronzed chest painted with symbols and blue wampum beads around his neck and wrists. He was a splendid dignified figure.

'It is time. The sun is at its zenith. It must be now. You will come?'

'Of course, Chief. I also want to thank you for what you have done.'

'I have done nothing. It is you who have done much. You are the one who vanquished the one who endangered our sacred place. For that we are now indebted to you now and always. Come.'

Maria helped Tumbleweed to climb the few steps to the sacrificial ledge. He was startled to see a great multitude down below and as far as he could see the plain on the valley floor was a seething colourful mass of Indians packed tightly together. While overhead, somewhere hidden from his sight, was a drummer who beat a tattoo on a leather skin drum which called and echoed around the valley drawing ever more Indians to the crowd.

Then, when his eyes got used to the glare he saw the fire blazing. Great tongues of flame licking at a white goat which already had its throat cut. He sighed with relief.

He'd had the idea that Ramsey might be used as a sacrifice and he'd not dared ask Maria because she too was primitive in her thinking.

The smell of roasting goat came in waves. Cochicata advanced to the very edge of the great ledge and raised both arms to heaven and his deep resonant voice chanted prayers to the great sun god. The sun was overhead and the rays and heat poured down from above bringing out the sweat.

Then Cochicata turned swiftly, his cloak swinging all about him and he took Tumbleweed by the hand and led him to the centre of the great ledge. He lifted his arm and presented him to the people and a great roar went up. It was so intense that to Tumbleweed's fevered imagination it was like the roar of an animal.

'What goes on?' he managed to mutter.

'You are the saviour of our sacred place and you are one of us now. All you have to do now is rid us once and for all time, of the evil that is still amongst us.'

'What must I do?'

'You will drive the devil from off this ledge.'

'But the sacrifice is burning! The goat...'

Cochicata laughed and it sounded like the

growl in the great multitude beast's throat. Tingles went up and down Tumbleweed's spine.

'The goat is but a symbol, a gesture to the people. The real evil is the white man. You must drive him over the cliff!'

Cochicata turned and gestured behind him and Tumbleweed looked and saw the travesty that was once Quantrill's trusted lieutenant, now a hunched punch-drunk hunk of meat.

'But I can't just herd him over the edge! It's not the white man's way. It would be murder!'

Cochicata looked at him with smiling puzzlement.

'But you have already killed him in his mind. He has already faced his destiny and he knows the time has come for him to atone. You must help him on his way. That is all. Come, you may talk to him but make it quickly. The people are getting restless for the feasting that will come later.'

Cochicata's grip was firm and hard as he led Tumbleweed to where Ramsey was standing. He saw that he was tied by a rawhide rope to a ring embedded in the slab of rock which served as an altar.

The man stared at him, his eyes empty

and Tumbleweed grew suspicious for he was sure that he was drugged.

'The drums! All I hear are the drums! They accuse me and sentence me over and over again. I want to be free! For God's sake man, just get this over and done with quick!'

'What do you want me to do?'

'A quick bullet would be merciful. I can't stand the drums plucking at my brains. It's an agony.'

'I swore I'd never let you have it quick. I said you should suffer...'

'For God's sake, I am suffering!'

'Then I'll free you and you may suffer forever!'

Quickly Tumbleweed unloosed the bonds and Ramsey rubbed his chafed wrists and then he said wildly, 'If I run, will you kill me? Make a good job of it?'

'I don't know. You will have to wait and see!'

Ramsey gave a strangled cry and ran for the stairs and stopped abruptly as Cochicata barred the way. With another cry he turned and ran towards the ledge with Cochicata following.

Tumbleweed too moved towards the ledge, a confused idea of holding him prisoner for he wanted to take Ramsey back to San Paulo and further shame.

He reached out for Ramsey but Ramsey's leap into space took him far out beyond any help. His kicking struggling body hurtled downwards and the press of people down below drew back and Ramsey hit the ground.

Tumbleweed looked around. Maria was standing with a blazing look of elation on her face. He felt sick. She was a primitive all right and now he knew the answer to her tentative proposal. Her bed would never know his presence. He would never take up Cochicata's offer of becoming a blooded Indian. He would always be a wandering soul, looking for what he might never find.

He didn't even want to go back to San Paulo and report Ramsey's death and, as for the bank roll, it would help Maria and Cochicata's band to survive. After all, Shawcross was crooked too and that bloody sheriff of his and perhaps everyone in San Paulo and so to hell with them all!

He walked over to Maria who looked up at him pleadingly.

'We could have a good life together, Tumbleweed.' But she saw his decision in his eyes.

He touched her mouth with his and

tenderly ran his finger under her eyes where lay the tears.

'I'm sorry, Maria. I'm Tumbleweed by name and tumbleweed by nature. It wouldn't work out, sweetheart. Some day I should break out and I'd hurt you and I'd be gone. Better to leave now while we like and respect each other. You'll find a much better man for yourself than me.'

He turned to leave and he paused at the stairhead and looked at Cochicata who was haranguing the crowd below. He smiled.

'Give him my regards and thank him for the honour.' He turned and went down the stairs. He didn't see her cry or hear the words she whispered after him.

'Goodbye, Tumbleweed. I'll never forget you. Some day you might come back and there might be two of us waiting...'

This Large Print Book, for people
who cannot read normal print,
is published under the auspices of

THE ULVERSCROFT FOUNDATION